CHARLIE MESSINA \
REPORT HAVING S
DECEASED DAUGHTER JUNI, AND IT ....
DOG NAMED DUMBASS. HIS WIFE AND SONS THINK
HE'S LOST HIS MIND.

Photographer and retired college professor Charlie Messina, seventy-five and weary of a long life behind the veil (he was born with a caul) is led through a redemptive understanding of parallel time by some unsuspecting children—and a supposedly imaginary dog. In addition to his family, the cast of characters who travel along with Charlie on his odyssey back and forth through time and space—as well as real or imagined journeys to Madison, Wisconsin, Sanibel Island and Key West, Florida--include nine year old Joey, whom he meets at a lobster roll stand on Cape Cod; fifteen year old Manny who works at his father's Sunoco gas station in Newport; Manny's father Raul, who threatens Charlie with a tire iron; Charlie's longtime friend and part-time nemesis Mason, a big band Lothario; and arguably most important, a fat old dog he's named Dumbass.

What Readers Are Saying About The Lights Around the Shore

"...wildly imaginative and entertaining...you'll be thinking about Charlie and his family long after you finish this book. A must read."—*Tony Hozeny, author of Driving Wheel and* My House Is Dark

"...this extraordinary book transports us through mysteries of perception where time, logic and even death prove more fluid than we think. Take this journey!"—*Irene O'Garden, Off-Broadway playwright, award-winning poet, and author of Glad to Be Human*

"...Lewis is a wit master, the giver of hilarious dialogue and an experimental approach to storytelling that unveil the preciousness of Charlie's gifts-the seen and unseen ones-and offer them space and time to shine on each captivating page."—*Kathy Curto, author of Not for Nothing: Glimpses into a Jersey Girlhood*

i

Excerpt

Moments later, after the air in the studio has gone still, the two of them breathless, Charlie murmurs, "And then, wouldn't you know it, the damn mutt showed up at the back door yesterday!"

Turning his head from side to side, then quickly glancing back toward the kitchen, Dylan whispers, "Dog? Where's the dog?"

"I guess you can't see it."

"I can't see it."

"Right. You can't see it. But I'm not crazy, son. I'm just finding out that once you step through a veil, you can see things that were hidden in all those gauzy layers that keep us cocooned. Things that were always there but just never noticed. You know what I mean?"

"Yeah. No. I guess." Dylan scans stares out through the window into the marsh. "You do know I can't see a dog."

"Yes, Dylan."

"So where is it?"

"Right here," Charlie says, pointing to the side of his shoe. "And now you're looking at me like you're really afraid I'm crazy."

Dylan's flat smile grows toothy. "Well, you're right, I am definitely afraid that you're crazy, Dad. Batshit loony tunes, if you really want to know." He presses his lips together, then adds, "But I have to say that I almost kind of like it. After the last how many years? Batshit loony tunes would be a relief."

THE LIGHTS AROUND THE SHORE

Steven Lewis

Moonshine Cove Publishing, LLC
Abbeville, South Carolina U.S.A.
First Moonshine Cove Edition Aug 2021

ISBN: 9781952439148

Library of Congress LCCN: 2021913805

Dedication

For Patti. "Into the company of love / it all returns."
(Robert Creeley)

Acknowledgment

Enduring thanks to my faithful, smart, honest readers along the way, each of whom let me know when and where I was going off the rails on this fast moving adventure between here and now: Mihai Grunfeld, Karen Dukess, Richard Kollath, Richard Corozine, Julie Evans, Joanna FitzPatrick, and my first reader always, Patti Lewis.

To Ed McCann, Kathy Curto, Irene O'Garden, and Tony Hozeny, uncommonly good friends and superb writers whose remarkable lives elevate my days and whose words enhance the cover of this book.

To Marjorie Weiss, dear old friend and brilliant artist, whose beautiful image graces the front cover of this book.

To Jim Russek, dear old friend and brilliant designer, who took Marjorie Weiss's stunning image and turned it into a book cover

At a time when a formulaic approach to writing too often rules the day in "legacy" publishers, deep appreciation for Moonshine Cove Publishers who are committed to publishing good books in whatever form they take.

About the Author

Steve Lewis lives in New York's Hudson River Valley. He is a former Mentor at SUNY-Empire State College, current member of the Sarah Lawrence College Writing Institute  faculty, and longtime freelancer. His work has been published widely, from the notable to the beyond obscure, including The *New York Times, The Washington Post, Christian Science Monitor, LA Times, Ploughshares, Narratively, Spirituality & Health, Road Apple Review, The Rosicrucian Digest,* and a biblically long list of parenting publications (7 kids, 16 grandkids).

Senior Editor/Literary Ombudsman for the spoken word podcast Read650.org, his book list includes *Zen and the Art of Fatherhood, Fear and Loathing of Boca Raton, If I Die Before You Wake* (poems), three recent novels, *Take This,* a generational sequel, *Loving Violet,* and *A Hard Rain,* all from Codhill Press. *Fire in Paradise,* a collection of poems with his daughter, Elizabeth Bayou Grace, is forthcoming in 2021.

www.stevenlewiswriter.com

PART I

Now whatever is this red water, boss, just tell me! An old stock grows branches, and at first there's nothing but a sour bunch of beads hanging down. Time passes, the sun ripens them, they become as sweet as honey, and then they're called grapes. We trample on them; we extract the juice and put it into casks; it ferments on its own, we open it on the feast day of St. John the Drinker, it's become wine! It's a miracle! You drink the red juice and, lo and behold, your soul grows big, too big for the old carcass, it challenges God to a fight. Now tell me, boss, how does it happen?

—Nikos Kazantzakis, *Zorba the Greek*

CHAPTER ONE: TOWARD THE END OF JUNE

Charlie Messina, seventy-five and sick and tired of it all, dropped a squishy handful of overripe blueberries into the bowl of Special K and, glancing beyond the jar of honey, reached for the sugar. Spooned in two overflowing tablespoons. Then a splash from the quart container of 2% on the counter. Then another splash. Then a few glug-glugging dribbles to top it off.

He slipped the *Globe* under his armpit, picked up the bowl in one meaty hand and a cup of coffee in the other, walked around the kitchen island, and sat down at the farm table across from his wife Sarah. She had her bronze-colored coffee and was reading something on her iPad, the morning sun over the salt marsh making her squint. BadBreath, their old and fat German shepherd mix, was snoring under the table. Sarah didn't look up, even after Charlie stared at her for a few seconds before picking up his spoon.

Of course, Charlie knew how to hold a spoon properly, but he had recently taken to holding it like convicts in grade B movies, shoveling the cereal into his mouth as if it were gruel.

Four or five shovelfuls in, he glanced down at the *Globe*: nothing but disheartening headlines about that jackass in the White House and his tawdry friends and family. Then he glanced up, beyond Sarah, toward his studio and the dozens of prints he was supposed to be preparing for his retrospective at Salve Regina.

He pushed the bowl of cereal away. "I gotta get outa here," he

Sarah finally raised her eyes. "Well, it's about time. You've been moping around this house for weeks. Go out and enjoy the day; it looks like it's going to be beautiful."

"A lot you know," he said, then quickly smiled his boyish Charlie smile.

"I know a lot more than you."

"You weren't born with a caul."

She closed her eyes. It was an old conversation. A really old conversation. One she was no longer interested in pursuing. "I might not have been born with a caul, Charlie Messina ... and I might not know a lot," she went on, still smiling, though a bit flatter now, "but I know you, you old coot, and I know you're not doing me any favors staying home and sneering at everything, caul or no caul."

Charlie shoveled up another spoonful of the cereal and, a moment later, with his mouth full, said, "Was that supposed to help?"

Now Sarah's smiling lips grew thinner. *I'm not going to talk to you anymore*, they said.

"Okay, you win," he muttered. "I'm outa here." He pushed back the chair and stood. Sarah silently toodle-ooed him with her fingers as he leaned over and asked BadBreath if he wanted to go for a ride.

The old dog lifted his load, stretched, and followed, wagging his thick tail, into the garage. To the old used-to-be-white Jeep. After Charlie opened the half door, BadBreath somehow managed to will his front paws up to the torn upholstery, then waited for his rear end to be hoisted up to the seat. Then waited again for Charlie to walk around the back of the Jeep, slide in on the other side, and reach across into the glove box for a Milk-Bone. And with drool and crumbs falling on the seat, the two old friends backed out of the barn, the engine wheezing, on to Ledge Road.

At the corner of Bellevue, Charlie braked toward the STOP sign but was still rolling as he entered the quiet intersection, looking right then left. "Right? Left?" he said to the dog before coming to a halt halfway across the road.

BadBreath stared at him like he was pathetic or invisible.

"Right. What the hell does it matter?"

Charlie yanked the wheel right, riding the clutch around the turn, lurching into a bucking third, and was soon in full conversation with himself, though it might have looked to an outsider that he was talking to the dog. He was thinking about his sons, Dylan and Andrew, and wondering if he should just drop in on one or the other. "Neither of them," he said, his voice trailing off before stating the obvious.

Following Bellevue around the curve, Charlie began humming "King of the Road." And with that, he reached into the open glove box for the pack of Lucky Strikes he kept there so Sarah wouldn't bug him about quitting. Like the song, though, the carton was empty, flat, and crumpled.

BadBreath lifted his snout and stared at Charlie, full of what Charlie interpreted as anticipation. He reached farther over and got his sweet, overweight boy another Milk-Bone.

And that was that. Until he had to jam on the brakes at the red light at Ruggles Road.

When the light turned green he drove right past the frame shop, past where he should have turned for the post office, past the hospital, moving mindlessly north, left, right, signaling a right on East Main, soon headed out of town on 138. He passed the Lowe's even though he needed a new drill and kept going as the old Jeep rumbled through Fall River.

New Bedford.

Wareham.

In Sandwich, unaccountably famished, he stopped at his favorite weathered joint, Gertie's Roadside Rest, for a lobster roll and a Coke. He waited to take that first luscious bite until after he'd hoisted himself up on the warm hood and breathed in the early summer breezes on the Cape, which always—spring, summer, fall, winter—felt fresher than the marshy air around Newport.

And after the first bite, his mouth full, Charlie held his lobster roll up to the heavens and said, "Goddamn that is good!"

"What?" came a young, girly voice off to the side.

Charlie looked over at an eight- or nine-year-old boy sitting on a rusty bike next to him. Mop of dirty blond hair. Freckles. Looked like he stepped out of Mark Twain's head.

"Wasn't talking to you," Charlie grunted, but he smiled his kindly smile because the kid looked scared. 'Sorry, kid … I was talking to myself."

"Y'know, you shouldn't use the Lord's name in vain, mister." The boy leaned back on his long banana bicycle seat, just in case.

Charlie frowned. He was about to tell the kid to bug off, but with nothing ahead, he figured this might be momentarily entertaining. "Why not?" He smirked and opened his mouth wide to take in a dripping mouthful of the lobster roll.

The kid pointed to his chin. Charlie narrowed his eyes, then understanding, wiped his short, white beard on his shoulder. "Why not?" he said again, his mouth still full of the pink meat.

"Want a nakkin?"

"No." Charlie wiped his chin on his shoulder again. "Why not?"

"Why not what?"

"Why not take the Lord's name in vain?"

"My mom says so. It ain't right." The boy's eyes grew wide then, and he backed up the bike a few steps.

Charlie looked over his shoulder. BadBreath had woken out of his slumber and sat up on the passenger seat. He was panting, drooling, eyes now fixed on Charlie's outstretched hand. "He's harmless, kid. Old and fat. Like me. Name's BadBreath. Not me, my breath is minty clean." Then pointing, "Him."

"He's big, B-I-G," was all the kid, still wide-eyed, could muster.

"Yeah, big, but like I said, old and fat like someone I know very well—or, as it turns out, maybe not well at all. Anyway, why not?"

The boy narrowed his eyes. "Why not what?"

"What'll happen if I take the Lord's name in vain?"

The boy shrugged and turned the rusted handlebars as if he were about to ride away. "Dunno."

Charlie held up his free hand like a crossing guard. "Just wait a minute, young man. I got another question for you. What do you mean you don't know? You don't think for yourself?"

Now it was the kid's turn to frown. "I dunno," he said, and moments later he flashed a sheepish grin. "I guess I'm too young to be thinkin' for myself."

Charlie laughed, his first laugh of the day. Maybe the week. He tore off the bottom end of the lobster roll and held it out. "You hungry?"

"Not for that."

"No? This is the best damn lobster roll on the Cape. I know."

"Not if ya gotta eat 'em all the time." The boy puffed out his cheeks like he was going to throw up.

Charlie felt his eyes narrow, slowly assembling the story that was unfolding before him. "So is Gertie your grandma?"

The boy laughed. "Noooooo, there ain't no Gertie, mister. Mr. Chet Williams owns the place. My mom works for him."

He was still smirking when a tired looking woman in a baseball cap, thick blond ponytail flopping out behind, leaned out of the sliding window and yelled, "Joey! Leave the nice man alone." Then she glanced up at Charlie: "Sorry, sir. He's—"

Charlie held up the hand with the part of the roll he'd offered to Joey: "He's no bother, ma'am." He was going to add that her son was about to tell him why he shouldn't take the Lord's name in vain, but figured that might get the kid in trouble.

"Well, you let me know if he starts botherin' you. He will."

When she disappeared behind the sliding window, Charlie slid down off the front of the Jeep, lumbered over to the passenger door, and gave the chunk of lobster roll to BadBreath. Then he turned back to the boy, who was then leaning on the handlebars, his cheek pressed onto his hands.

"Shouldn't you be in school?"

Joey didn't lift his head. "Summer vacation."

The old man frowned. "Right. What the hell was I thinking, right?"

"Not s'posed to say that word, either."

Charlie waved him off. "You're a pip, kid. You like school?"

The boy raised his eyebrows and tilted his head like that was the stupidest question he had ever heard.

"Stupid question, right?" The kid, his head still resting on his arms, nodded. "You hungry?"

The boy's eyes shifted up toward the last of the lobster roll, and he puffed out his cheeks.

Charlie laughed again. "No, I meant something else. You want an ice cream or something?" He arched his back and, sliding a thick hand into his pocket, found some folded bills; he plucked out a five and held it out.

The boy sat up. Licked his lips. "Might," he said, lifting his leg over the bike and letting it drop onto the gravel. A moment later he was reaching up and trying to snatch the bill out of Charlie's outstretched fingers, but the old man pulled it back before the boy could snag it.

"I'm paying for information, Joey."

The boy looked confused. Charlie held the bill up again and watched him bend over to pick up his bike, swing his leg over the back tire, and sit down on the ripped seat. He lifted his right foot to the pedal.

"Hey, where you going?"

"I dunno. Somewhere, I guess," the kid said, pointing up the road.

"Don't you want ice cream?"

"I got no money, mister—and I ain't got no infertation, whatever that means."

"In-for-*may*-shun, kid ... the score, the scoop, the lowdown, the inside story." Joey shook his head with each new definition. "Okay, I get it. So, let's just cut to the chase. Do they have ice cream here?" Charlie waved the bill over the boy's head.

"My mom, she wouldn't let me."

Charlie nodded. "Gotcha," he said, poking the last bit of roll into his mouth and swallowing it whole like a dog.

"So where else can someone get ice cream around here?"

Twisting around and pointing up Route 6 toward Sandwich, Joey whispered, "Ben and Jerry's."

"Okay. Well, I'm gonna get you some ice cream up there. But first you owe me an explanation."

Joey's eyes narrowed. "What did I do?"

"Nothing. I just want to know why I shouldn't take the Lord's name in vain. I think I've been taking the Lord's name in vain my whole life. Maybe I should find out why it's not a good thing. Should be worth five bucks." He held out the fiver again. "What I want to know is why in vain?"

The kid shrugged. "I dunno, something to do with the weather."

That brought a guffaw. "That's your answer?"

The kid shrugged again, plucked the bill out of the old man's outstretched hand, and, seconds later, rear tire fishtailing on the gravel, pedaled off like he was escaping the Boogie Man.

Charlie watched the boy disappear around the bend; watched the traffic on Route 6 whiz by for a minute or two; saw what he thought was a red-tailed hawk sailing on the thermals. Then he shrugged, wiped his palms on his stained khakis, grabbed his garbage and the Coke, slid off the hood, and with a grunt hoisted himself back into the driver's seat.

First, he undid the two ragtop latches and flipped the contraption over his head. Listened for the comforting wheeze as he backed up and spun around on the gravel. Ground the gears, jamming the stick into first. Headed up 6 in the direction the kid had pointed.

A half mile or so up the road, he saw the Ben and Jerry's in a strip mall. The rusted bike was down on the sidewalk in front of the big window.

From the rumbling Jeep, where the windshield vibrated, the old man could see Joey in the back of the small shop, sitting alone at one of those round ice cream–parlor tables. A teenage girl in the pink Ben and Jerry's baseball hat was bringing him what looked like a small hot-fudge sundae. Joey didn't look up, even as Charlie stared intently at him through the two windows trying in vain to command or conjure his attention.

Charlie shrugged, put the Jeep into reverse—the wheeze reminding him of the out-of-tune organ at the roller rink near his childhood home in Milford, Connecticut—backed out onto the shoulder, signaled, and, merging easily into the light afternoon traffic, headed back home to Newport. To the studio. To Sarah.

Through Wareham.

Through New Bedford.

Through Fall River.

Just as he approached the Newport line, Charlie leaned across the dog's snout to pluck a cigarette out of the glove box, found the empty pack again and remembered, crunched it up this time, and threw it on the floor.

And a quarter mile after the rotary in Newport, he pulled into a Sunoco station for a pack of Luckies.

CHAPTER TWO: LESS THAN A MINUTE LATER

Before bellying up to the counter, Charlie scanned the cigarette display on the back wall to make sure there were Lucky Strikes up there. They were getting harder and harder to find anywhere.

The teenager behind the register, plaid short-sleeve shirt buttoned to the neck, buzz cut, pimples, ears still too big for his narrow head, looked up, smirked, and said, "And what can I do for you, young man?" He raised his thick eyebrows as if the two of them were sharing a private joke.

Charlie glowered at the boy, maybe fifteen, maybe seventeen. He pointed a thick finger across the counter. "Don't patronize me, kid."

The boy's hands flew up in the air in instant surrender—his smile transformed into a dark circle out of which came a squeaky voice. "I'm sorry, mister, I'm sorry, I didn't mean—"

Charlie saw what he had done. He moved his pointing finger up and turned it into a spread palm, interrupting the boy's continued pleading. "Stop!" he said more softly.

The boy pressed his lips together. Moments later, though, he opened his mouth like he was going to start apologizing again.

"No. Don't say a word!" Charlie's hand was still up. "I'm the one that should be saying sorry."

Now the kid looked catatonic. His Adam's apple moved up and down.

Charlie took a deep breath through his nostrils and slowly let it out. "Listen, I've had a bad day, a bad year, a bad few years, eighteen of 'em if you want to know. I had no business getting smart with you."

The boy remained still, moving his eyes back and forth as if he was looking for someone. Charlie figured it might be his boss, who might fire him for being rude to a customer. Charlie lowered his hand and spoke out of the side of his mouth: "Don't worry, kid, I'm not going to get you in trouble."

With his eyes still wide, the boy nodded. He parted his lips again, but no sound came out, just a swath of crooked teeth.

"Y'know, you could use some braces."

The boy pressed his lips together.

"Sorry. I was just lightening the air. Or trying to. Didn't mean—well, okay ... just get me, no ... *please* get me a pack of Luckies."

After the cigarettes and money were exchanged—after Charlie stopped himself before carping about the price of cigarettes *these days*—and after the Luckies were stowed safely in his breast pocket, Charlie turned away and was heading out the door when he figured he owed the kid, still wide-eyed, still tight lipped, some better explanation. He turned back.

His finger was up in the air again. "Y'know, it really wasn't a bad day, kid. In fact, there were a couple of things that happened that I think were pretty good, but"—he paused then and felt for the cigarettes— "but, well, I'm not going to go into it. You don't need to know any of it, not that it's your business or that you'd care." He breathed in and out through his nostrils again. "But I've been going through a rough patch lately about ... well, I'm not going to go into it, but when you made that"—air quotes—"joke and I, y'know, I just flew off the handle. You know what that means?"

The boy nodded. It was clear he had no idea what Charlie was talking about.

"Anyway, I'm sorry."

The boy nodded again. The blood was back in his head, but there were beads of sweat on his forehead.

"Just for the record, though ..." Charlie waited until the kid nodded his head one more time. "Just for the record, kid, don't ever call any adult—you know what I mean, a senior citizen—"young man" again. God knows what some of us will do." He drew his finger across his throat with a self-deprecating smirk.

The boy nodded one more time, a smile flickering at the corners of his mouth.

Just then the glass door opened behind Charlie, and a man in grease-stained blue mechanic's clothes, skinny ponytail drooping out the back of his cap, walked behind the counter. "Hey, yo, Manny," he said, "your old man needs you in Bay One."

Manny looked at Charlie, and Charlie motioned *Go* with his head. Moments later Charlie followed Manny out of the gas station convenience store and stopped just outside the bay. He waited until the kid's father looked up from underneath the hood of a Chevy Caprice. "I just want to tell you that Manny is doing a great job."

The man tilted his head. Then he looked at his son as if to say *What the hell is that all about?*

A few seconds later, Raul Cardozo nodded at Charlie and then glanced back down under the hood. He picked up a socket wrench in one hand and, without looking up, handed it to his son. "Get me a ten millimeter." Charlie thought he could hear a Portuguese cadence in between the syllables.

Manny said, "Yes, Papa," walked over to the toolbox, made the switch, and walked back to his father, who reached blindly behind himself for the tool. But when Manny handed him the socket side instead of the handle, Cardozo growled, "The handle, Manny! What are you, some kind of donkey?"

"Sorry, Papa."

And a moment later, when the socket turned out to be the wrong size, Manny's father swung his arm back and hit the boy in the upper arm with the wrench. "Wrong size, goddamnit!"

The boy grabbed his arm and grimaced. The father held his arm behind him, still holding the wrench. "Take it, goddamnit! And give me the right one!"

Before he could stop himself, Charlie yelled from the doorway, "You don't want to be doing that."

Raul Cardozo stood up slowly and glared at him, still holding the wrench in his hand. "Who the fuck are you?" he said, no remnants of any Portuguese left on his tongue.

Charlie held up his hands, heart thudding. A second or two later, the question still pinballing around his mind, he shook his head and turned to walk away. "I don't know," he muttered to the ground.

Behind him, Cardozo was holding the wrench up in the air by the socket end. "That's right, you old fool, get the fuck out of here! And don't ever come back!"

Now Charlie didn't move. Wouldn't move. Couldn't move. Spread his feet more for balance than defiance.

"Get out before I call the cops."

Ashamed of himself, Charlie turned and walked back into the convenience store, and a few seconds later he was pushing open the glass door onto the sidewalk. His old Jeep was parked in the faded No Parking zone in front of the convenience store window. Charlie was still trembling when the engine rumbled to life and the car wheezed out of the station.

A half mile down Route 138 he grumbled to BadBreath, "If I was ten years younger, I'd a beat the living shit out of that piece of crap."

He reached into his breast pocket then and took out the pack of cigarettes, packed it down with a few thumps on the dashboard, looked appreciatively at the crisp lines of the bullseye and pulled over onto the side of the road.

He looked again at the red bullseye thinking, and not for the first time, *This is a talisman, a cross, a holy symbol* ... but as before, as ever, he had no idea why it was a talisman nor what it represented. And then began the daily mindless ritual, pulling the red cellophane tab, dropping the top of the cellophane on the floor, fingering open both tabs of the foil, and banging the open pack against his other palm.

He pulled out one cigarette.

Tamped it down on the dash.

Placed it in between his lips and sat still for a moment. Spit out a lone piece of tobacco stuck to his tongue and felt in his breast pocket for the matches. There were none, so he scrunched around and with a groan reached into his pants pocket. Nothing. Then the other one. Nothing. Then the glove box.

Not a goddamn match anywhere.

He made a U-turn, ground the gears, and headed back to the Sunoco station. Manny was back behind the counter. He watched the old man coming his way as if Charlie were a tornado.

Charlie saw again what he had done. Imagined the bruise on Manny's upper arm. "Don't worry, Manny—you can probably beat the crap out of me. And your old man can definitely knock the socks off of me." He smiled the old Charming Charlie smile, but Manny didn't get it, just stared at him, chest not moving. "But first you gotta breathe, son."

Manny nodded. But did not inhale.

"Take a breath, Manny. In through your nose, out through your mouth." Manny did. "Good. I'm just back here to get some matches." Then Charlie spied the Bic display. "I'm gonna take one of these, too," he said, pulling a cobalt blue one off the rack as Manny slid a pack of matches across the counter.

Charlie looked around. "You eat beef jerky?" Manny shook his head. "Apple pie?" Manny nodded, another fearful smile peeking out between his thin lips. "Well, I'm gonna buy you one—as penance. You know what penance is?"

Manny shrugged.

He took the pie slice and pushed it across the counter. "Penance is paying for your sins. An apology. Right?"

The kid nodded.

"Well, this piece of apple pie is my apology for getting in your face—and getting you in more trouble than you might have with your dad."

Manny shrugged again.

"What's a matter with you? You can't talk?"

"I can talk," the boy sputtered.

"That's good." The old man looked around and noticed the ice cream cooler. Walked over, slid open the door, reached in, pulled out a Häagen-Dazs ice cream bar, and tossed it on the counter. "I'm not even gonna ask if you like these. If you don't, there's something wrong with you."

"I like 'em."

"Of course, you do. Like 'em enough and they'll kill you someday, but for now ...." Charlie never finished the sentence. He reached into his pocket, pulled out a ten-dollar bill, and pushed it across the counter. "Just for the record, we're beyond penance now, Manny. I think the apple pie made us even. The ice cream is for pokin' my nose into your business, which I'm about to do right now."

Once again Manny clearly had no idea what the old guy was talking about. He made change for the apple pie and the ice cream bar and held it out. "Keep it," Charlie said, "I want some words ... what the hell was going on over there?" He pointed out toward the bays.

The kid looked scared again. "Nothing. I was just helpin' my dad."

"Does he talk to you like that all the time?"

Manny tilted his head back and forth. "No. Y'know, sometimes." He nodded. "Sometimes."

"Does he hit you?"

The boy shook his head in tight arcs.

"None of my business. Right?"

Manny scrunched up his lips and shrugged again. He pushed the change across the counter toward the old man. "Keep it," Charlie said. "And now I'll get out of here."

Manny didn't say anything, but Charlie still had more to say. "Just one thing, kid; you're not dumb. You're no donkey. I could see how smart you were as soon as I first walked into this joint."

Charlie figured that the smile Manny wore on his face looked painful beyond tears.

****

And that would've been that, another grumpy day in the grumpy old man's seventy-sixth year, if Sarah hadn't been around when he got home. She looked up from a book with a bright smile that barely hid her annoyance: "I was wondering where you were."

And then there was that thin veil in front of him, a membrane as delicate and transparent as a bubble separating him from answering Sarah's simple question. The same membrane that always appeared whenever she asked where he'd been, what he'd done, where he was going. For reasons he had never understood, he just didn't want to tell her. Didn't want to have to explain himself. Didn't want to be questioned. So, he gave her his usual "Oh, you know, everywhere, nowhere, you know, just running errands."

And that in turn would have been that ... the usual quiet scowl on her face as she'd begin reading again.

Except Nora Robinson had passed Charlie on Route 6 earlier in the day and mentioned it to Sarah, who was apparently not going to let it go this time. "What were you doing on Route 6?"

"Driving."

She folded the page at the top and put the book down. "What were you doing on Route 6, Charlie?"

He sneered, eyebrows reaching for his hairline. "Just like I said, I was just driving around."

"Where'd you go? Who'd you see? Who'd you talk to? Let's actually have a little conversation."

He didn't know why, but once again he couldn't force himself through that thin membrane of cordial impersonal talk that he'd manage so easily with almost anyone else. "You're pretty damn nosey for a good lookin' woman, you do know that, right?" He offered his best saccharine smile.

"I have to be."

So Charlie told her, in between loud nasal inhalations, about meeting some little kid at a lobster-roll joint on the Cape ... and the ice cream he'd bought for him up the road ... and then he told her about the other kid at the gas station, leaving out the part about getting into it with the boy's father.

"Poor kids," Sarah said.

Charlie wasn't sure whether she was kidding or not, but now, even as Sarah had rather quickly changed the subject to something or other about their oldest son, Dylan, Charlie was thinking that he wanted to go back to the Sunoco station. Had to go back. To photograph Manny ... and also that kid at the lobster-roll joint, Joey ... not that either of them was a particularly interesting or unique subject by himself. In fact, Charlie rarely photographed people, finding them predictably vain even when they didn't know they were being observed. But something about those two kids' unphotoshopped manner called to him.

The next morning he was out of the house with BadBreath before Sarah woke up, the old Hasselblad exchanged for the new digital Nikon in his bag, backing the Jeep slowly out of the garage with that comforting whine and, grinding the gears, heading back to the Sunoco in town.

Pulling up to the pumps, he could see Raul Cardozo gesturing angrily at the guy with the ponytail in the far bay. Manny was inside the shop, back behind the counter.

Charlie didn't actually need gas, but it was a decent and harmless excuse to get into the convenience store. As he imagined would happen, Manny's eyes grew wide when he saw Charlie push open the glass door and raise his hands in the air, a twenty between his pointer and middle fingers. "Just getting gas, kid. Put your eyes back in their sockets." Charlie placed the twenty on the counter and pushed it over to Manny. "Gimme twenty ... and hey," he said as if he had just thought of it, "would you mind if I take your picture?" He snatched the Nikon out of the black bag. "I'm a professional photographer."

He might as well have been aiming a Glock, judging by the horror on the boy's face. "I don't know," Manny sputtered. "I don't know."

"What do you mean you don't know? It's an easy yes or no question." Charlie held up the camera. "Doesn't shoot bullets."

Manny shook his head. "I don't know."

"You need to ask your old man?"

Manny shook his head again, now voiceless, his dark eyes turned down on the counter. He picked up the twenty.

"I'll go ask him," Charlie said and turned back.

"No!" And then in a whisper "I don't think that's a good idea, sir."

"Good ideas are way overrated. I just want to snap your picture. You need to put on a new shirt? Brush your teeth? Comb your hair?"

Manny smiled at the absurd questions. "No."

Now there was a smiling standoff. "So what? You come from some tribe that believes if I take your picture I'm gonna steal your soul?"

The boy shrugged and then opened the cash register. He slipped the twenty in the slot and pushed some button to reset the pump. "You're all set, sir."

"You didn't think that was funny?" Then pointing into the garage and taking a step like he was going to go in there, he said, "I feel like I gotta make things right with your old man. I'll make sure it's okay to take your picture."

"No. Please don't go in there."

"What's the harm?"

"I don't know. I don't know," Manny's dark eyes trained on the door to the bays. "He told me not to let you back in here. Said we didn't need your business."

"So, he's gonna beat you for disobeying him?"

Manny's mouth was a tiny circle now. "No," he whispered, "I don't know what he'll do ... to you."

"Me? I'm seventy-five years old. He's not gonna mess with a fat old man?"

Manny shrugged. "Please, mister."

"Nope." Charlie pressed his lips together. "Well, I know myself well enough to know I'm one toke over the line, sweet Jesus, and there's no coming back." And Manny watched wide-eyed as Charlie grabbed the knob, turned it, and strode into Bay 1.

Raul Cardozo had his back to Charlie and a tire iron in his hand. "Hey, you mind if I take some shots of your kid?" Charlie called out. He held up the camera.

Cardozo turned from the rack of tires. Glared like he had the day before, but it evidently took him a few moments to figure out who the old guy was. "Oh, it's you ... again," he said. "I thought I told you to get the fuck outa here yesterday."

Charlie lowered his chin onto his chest in what he hoped was a gesture of submission. "You did," he said, speaking to his shoes, "but it's a new day and"—he paused, waiting for the man to either speak or, worse, charge him—"and, I'd like to apologize for my big mouth yesterday. My wife tells me I'm a jackass." He paused to give the man a chance to say something. Maybe smile. "So does my oldest son. And my other son. That is, when they speak to me." Charlie flashed that half-mouthed smile that usually seems to charm Sarah or his old friend Mason when either of them is disgusted with him. Used to work on Joni, too. Not Dylan. Definitely not Andrew. At least not in the last eighteen years. Maybe before then, when he was the Good Time Charlie around Ledge Road.

Cardozo did not move, did not speak, so Charlie took that as a good sign and went on, still mumbling to the floor, "Big mouth gets me in trouble sometimes. But"—he looked up—"I'm still troubled by what I saw yesterday."

Now Cardozo took one step and pointed a grease-stained finger toward the street. "Get the fuck out of here!"

Both hands quickly in the air, Charlie leaned backward and grunted, "Sorry!" He flashed the now useless half grin. "Told you my big mouth gets me in trouble sometimes. I meant to say I think Manny is a great subject."

And when Cardozo again didn't move or say anything, Charlie went on: "I am a jackass, Mr. Cardozo. And to tell you the truth any time anyone told me what to do about my kids, all I wanted to do was shove my fist down their throats." He held up three fingers. "Three kids. Two boys and a girl." He closed his eyes. "She died eighteen years ago June." Shook his head, eyes glistening. Held back some unshed tears from the bottomless pit in his soul. "Tore me apart."

Then the two men were silent.

"Still does."

The ponytailed mechanic was over in the far corner of the garage, hands in his pockets, eyes wide and glassy; Charlie could feel Manny's anxious presence in the doorway behind him.

When the silence became unbearable, Charlie extended the camera to Cardozo. "So, now that we've agreed that I am a jackass, I also want you to know that I'm also a photographer." His voice tumbled an octave or two. "You know, a professional photographer—a good one, a really good one. I'm in museums and all that." And when that didn't seem to break through Cardozo's angry countenance, Charlie added, "And I teach, well, used to teach at the college"—he pointed in what he thought was the general direction of Salve Regina—"for more than forty years. Tenured and all that crap. And I want you to know that there's something about your son's countenance that needs to be recorded. I mean, he's a good kid at heart ... but of course you already know that."

Cardozo shook his head. Muttered, "Get out of here."

Charlie didn't move. Stood there wondering what would happen next, pins and needles in his fingers. He held the camera up and nodded, a smile flickering in one corner of his thin mouth. "I'm thinking of a series on him and a kid I met on the Cape a few days ago. I think it could be something great." He grinned again. "Make 'em both famous, like Norman Rockwell's kid." Big smile.

Cardozo stared at the old man. Dark piercing eyes. Shook his head again and turned his back. Framed in tires.

Charlie raised the camera and pressed the shutter. Click. Then again. Click. Then again. Click. Then he swirled around and aimed the lens at Manny in the doorway. Click. Manny in the doorway with his mouth open. Click. Manny, head turned toward his father. Click. Manny, head turned, eyes on Charlie. Click.

Charlie wheeled around then and, without another word, strode out of the open bay, waiting for a barrage of angry words or slapping footsteps or even a tire iron to come whirling through the air and smash the back of his head.

And in that extraordinary moment between breaths, Charlie thought that would've been okay, *My just desserts*. He was lurching out of the garage, striding toward the Jeep, sliding into the driver's seat, laying the camera down gently on the floor below BadBreath curled up on the passenger seat, stepping on the clutch, turning the key and pumping the gas pedal until there was a rumble and ignition, then easing up on the clutch, listening to the engine whine as the wheels turned, rolling out onto Main Street, thinking he got what he came for. His half smile flickered.

Ten minutes later, he was already out on Route 6, straining the engine, going twelve miles an hour above the speed limit, heading to the Cape, when he realized that he had forgotten to get the twenty dollars' worth of gas.

Of course, by then it was too late. And besides, he had gotten what he had come for. Nothing to do but just keep moving. "Just keep moving, Charlie," he grumbled to himself. "Keep moving through the curtain, BadBreath. Just one curtain after another."

CHAPTER THREE: EARLY AUGUST

"Charlie, Charlie, Charlie, will you please get out of the damn house? It's a beautiful summer day. I mean, for Christ's sake, get yourself some fresh air."

Charlie was in his studio, the wooden floor painted green, windows all around. He was on the same metal stool he'd been sitting on for decades, hunched over a large unmatted photograph, jeweler's magnifier in front of one eye. Without turning, he called back with no emotion, "I don't want to."

When he looked up, the device fell from his eye. He picked it up. Looked back toward the voice. Sarah was standing in the double doorway, facing the bank of windows that looked out onto the newly mowed yard and the salt marsh, hand in her massive tote feeling around for keys. "It's damn hot outside and I got work to do here." He felt for the Luckies in his breast pocket. They weren't there. "And where the hell would I go, anyway?"

Sarah was still fumbling around in the tote when she answered: "Well, you'll feel better, you old goat … and you'll stop being so damn grumpy. I mean, make some friends."

Charlie wasn't sure whether she found her keys or she was playing with him… or, after all these years, whether she was really, truly, and honestly as perky as she seemed to be most of the time, at least with other people. *Not that she didn't have her dark moments,* he was quick to tell all those pain-in-the-ass friends who would tell him how lucky he was to be married to such a beautiful, happy woman who didn't seem to age (like he had, they neglect to add).

"You are gorgeous," he said, smiling. He meant it.

She rolled her eyes. "Thank you very much. But that doesn't change anything, you know. You've been moping around for weeks, worse than usual. Ever since BadBreath died." She might have said for eighteen years; she might have even said for most of their entire forty-six-year marriage. But after all this time together, she knew to keep things close at hand with her husband. "Kinda like training a dog," she had long, long ago told their daughter, Joni.

He glared at her. "What moping? I'm grieving," he said, a failed smirk flickering at the corners of his mouth. "That dumbass dog was the only one in this whole damn family— maybe the whole world, for that matter—who loved and accepted me for who I am, warts and all." And before she had a chance to come back at him, he added, "And that "all" includes my rolls of fat, my big mouth, my bad manners, my inappropriate style of dress. All of it. And just for the record, as you well know, it's all because of—" He stopped himself, closed his eyes.

When he opened them, he saw that she had closed her eyes. "You know that's only half the story, not even half the story, in fact—"

He cut her off. "Besides, I'm working. I'm doing some of the best work of my life." He put the magnifying glass down on the table and held up two large-scale black-and-white photographs, one of BadBreath he'd taken in June, a few weeks before Sarah insisted they put the "poor suffering dog down," the other of a young boy on a red bicycle, a field of junipers in the background. Charlie slid the photo of BadBreath back onto the table and turned the one of the boy toward Sarah.

"Very nice, Charlie. But do us all a favor and go find a friend. Someone your own age." She pulled out the ring of keys, half a dozen plastic store bar codes, a tiny Swiss Army knife. "Why don't you call up Mason and go visit. I'm sure he'd love to see you."

Mason, a retired music professor at Brown and itinerant drummer for various orchestras, cruise ship and otherwise, had been Charlie's college roommate at Williams. "Mason doesn't want to see me. I've tried. He's got his own stuff going, not the least of which is a wasted existence bent on bedding widows on cruise ships."

She raised her eyebrows and shook her head. Forced a smile. "Well, I gotta go—book group." She shook the keys, smiled again, and turned to go. Then turned back, Lauren Bacall fashion, and said, "Why don't you give Mason a whistle—you know how to whistle, don't you, Charlie?"

"If I knew why the sonofabitch hates me so goddamn much, that might be a good start."

She shook her head in mock or mocking disgust—he couldn't tell. "Maybe you two can find a way to be friends again. Or go make some new friends. Anyway, stop moping." After pausing as if deciding whether to go on, she blurted out, "And let me tell you, if I ever bought that ridiculous crap about the caul, which I didn't and I don't, you should know that bus probably left the station decades ago." She took a deep breath in through her nostrils and out her mouth. "And definitely after Joni—" But she didn't finish, turned, and walked out of the sunny studio.

"Train!" he called out, correcting her, but she didn't take the bait. He heard footsteps and then the refrigerator door slam shut. "I'm not your son." he yelled. Then to no one, his palms turned up, glancing beyond the lawn to the salt marsh, "I'm not your son."

Then he was thinking about Joni, the delight of his life, at least until the light went out. Then Dylan, whom he hadn't heard from in five or six months. And now the photograph was blurry.

The morning's bowl of Special K growing soggy and soggier next to the keyboard, Charlie clicked on Facebook. More damn photos of kids and dogs and photoshopped marvels of nature. Poor Enid threatening to kill herself. Again. Peter whining on and on about the school board. Justine and Robert promoting their landscaping business. Carlton with his daily bashing of the NRA. Gloria with her simpy, saccharine, damaging feel-good sayings with unicorns and rainbows. Maureen, the former free-love hippie, now an Ayn Rand devotee, decrying the global warming fraud.

And then there was Sarah again, calling from the kitchen that she was leaving and wouldn't be back til dinner.

"I thought you already left," he said after he heard the door close. Now full of the old remorse. Unable to escape the feeling that Sarah was just tired of him, down to the bone, as annoyed with him as he was with himself, maybe even more annoyed at being annoyed at his ways all these years. "Wears you down," he whispered. In any case, he knew in his heart that he was not the man she'd hoped he might become back when they were running around naked in Berkeley. Not the husband or dad she expected him to be after Andrew was born. Or Dylan. Or Joni. "A curmudgeon" they all call him when they're being nice—Sarah and Dylan and Andrew, anyway. And probably everyone who ever knew him at Salve Regina. But not Joni. "She got me," he whispered.

He clicked on Aperture. At least Sarah was still by his side. Couldn't tell why exactly, but he knew that fact was terribly important. And he loved her. And he thought she loved him. In her way.

After staring at the screen for a full minute, maybe more, Charlie moved the cursor up to the apple, clicked on Shut Down, and watched as the icons disappeared from the screen, then the whole thing went silver gray, then black.

***

He dropped the jeweler's glass on the work table, groaned as he pushed himself up, and went into the kitchen. Wiped his eyes with his sleeve. There was coffee still in the pot, but the automatic shut-off, which Sarah had demanded after her sister's kitchen caught on fire, had turned the machine off two hours ago. He felt the pot—cool. Poured a cup. Scooped in some sugar. Eyed the microwave but decided he wasn't willing to wait and took a big cool unsatisfying swig.

No matter what Sarah thought, it was all about the caul, the alpha and omega of his existence.

Nearly sixty years ago he swaggered into Sage Hall at Williams as a freshman, the vision of American optimism, tall, handsome, athletic, a ready smile, and for good measure, a chipped tooth. Backup for the starting linebacker as a freshman. A Good Time Charlie they called him.

But he soon found himself kind of morose in the spaces between classes, between football games, between fraternity mixers; that is, whenever he left his "sanctuary" in the dark room in Spencer Studio Art Building. Whatever the reason, he never felt at home at Williams. And other than Mason, whose friendship he didn't understand, Charlie was not close to anyone in the dorm or the Art Department or the football team. And going home to Milford on vacation was even worse. Milford no longer felt like home, if it ever had. It never did again.

It was coming back to Williams after that first Thanksgiving when Charlie decided it was the caul. The separateness. The sadness. One of his early memories ... their dog Billy giving birth to a pup in a sac, his mother, countering his disgust, explaining how he was also born in a caul—a veil, a thin amniotic sac—just like the puppy, his grandmother nodding and smiling, whispering "Camicia," both of them telling him how that made him special. Protected. *"Non annegherai mai,"* Nonna said. "You'll never drown," Mama translated with an angelic smile.

And after that, his late mother, the former Valentina Rosa Giovanni of Assisi, had often told him—in her own broken English—that it made him special. And then she always crossed herself.

His late father, Pasquale Messina, never bought it. "He's not so special, Tina. He's just a spoiled, lazy American boy."

And thereafter, he never mentioned it again. Or thought about it. Until he got back to Williams after Thanksgiving and sat alone in his dorm room, staring up at the shadows on the ceiling, wondering if he was fated to always feel separate from everyone.

Everyone, that is, except Sarah, whom he met at a Holyoke mixer—and who somehow broke through the thin veil. He still didn't know how it had happened. Or why she had tried. "Something about you," Sarah used to tell him back then, with one of four or five different inflections depending on how lovable or flat-out annoying he was being at the moment.

And then there was Joni. Until there wasn't.

And, at times, his nominal best friend—and roommate—Mason. Mason skipped the charming part and had been telling him for more than half a century that he was a major pain in the ass, which morphed occasionally into "You're a goddamn pain in the ass, Charlie Messina, so fuck you, you fucking fuck of a pain in my ass."

Worse, Charlie knew in his heart—had known for seemingly forever—that breaking through that thin membrane would be as easily accomplished as reaching out and tearing a hole in it. Could've done it back when he was fourteen, eighteen. One rip, one step across the veil, and he could march right into the promised land. The arms of his wife and children. Happiness.

Whatever the promised land was promising.

But he had never really walked through the veil, except with Sarah, and mostly when they were making love. And that was something altogether different.

And with Joni, although that was wholly different and holy.

The only thing that was clear was that after Joni died, the caul had just gotten thicker.

***

Now he was looking at the wall phone, staring at it, but before he could think to recite Mason's numbers, he walked out of the house and plucked a Lucky from his pocket, dug deep in his khakis for some matches, lit the cigarette, and inhaled deeply. Waved dismissively to Maureen Rogers, who drove by in her Range Rover and tooted her horn.

Five minutes later, he flicked the lit butt into a ditch, turned, stamped his shoes on the welcome mat, headed back into the kitchen, and went directly to the wall phone.

"Hello?"

"Hello, it's me, the asshole you love to hate. My wife says I need some fresh air." Charlie held his breath through the silence.

"First of all, jackass, I don't love to hate you—I hate you pure and simple, and I only hate you when you act like an asshole." Another silence. Some fumbling with the phone. "So, don't act like an asshole. And if you're asking if I'd like to get some fresh air with you, I'll give you a qualified yes. Let's say I'll pick you up in, say, fifteen minutes."

Charlie grimaced. "I'll pick you up. I already got the keys in my hand." He didn't.

"No. I'm not driving around Newport in that drafty piece of shit you call a car."

Now it was Charlie's turn to be silent. "Then I'm gonna smoke."

"Not in my car, you're not. There might be some people still alive who cower at your bullshit, Chuck, but not me. I had the misfortune of once living with you. I'll pick you up in fifteen minutes. Please give my regards to the long-suffering Sarah." A moment later Charlie heard the click, held the receiver away from his ear, and just stood there looking at the phone.

And fifteen minutes later a red Fiat Cabrio convertible pulled up in front of 17 Ledge Road. Mason tooted that fruity horn. Charlie already had his crumpled, sweat-stained Red Sox hat on and had his hand on the doorknob, but he sneered when he heard the beep and decided to make his old friend wait.

He counted, "One one thousand, two one thousand ...," and just as he reached his goal of "thirty-one thousand," the phone rang and Charlie walked back into the kitchen. "I'm out front," the familiar voice grumbled even before Charlie had a chance to say hello.

Charlie hung up without a word and then, after counting up to ten one thousand, walked out the door.

The Fiat still had the new car smell. Charlie put on his seat belt without a word. Mason smiled and patted him on the knee. "Good boy." And after a pause to let that sink in, he added, "I gotta say, Chuck, it's almost kinda sorta good to see you, old pal."

"That's not what you said last time I saw you."

Mason sneered, slid the shifter into first, and slowly let out the clutch, and they were off, second, third, braking at the stop sign. "That's because you were being an asswipe, if I remember correctly." He patted Charlie's knee again. "Some things never change, hah?"

"I don't remember, but it was probably because you were being the arrogant, womanizing jackass you've been since Williamstown."

Now they were turning on to Memorial Boulevard, both smiling to themselves. Charlie watched as Mason did something with his thumbs on the steering wheel, and Dvorak played in surround sound. "So ... like my new wheels?"

Charlie looked all around. "It looks like a bumper car—or one of those motorized toy things rich people buy for their five-year-olds to ride around the lawn." He smirked at his own joke and reached into his breast pocket for the pack of Luckies he had taken out of the Jeep.

"Put those damn things away—you are not smoking in my very sweet new ride."

"It's a girl's car." Charlie had the pack out now.

"Better than the dumbass Ronald Reagan faux cowboy piece of shit you use to hold on to your long, long, long, long gone virility."

"Let me outa here," Charlie said, knocking a cigarette loose from the pack. Grabbed it between his lips.

"Don't you fuckin' dare."

Now they were speeding along what Charlie often referred to as "the aptly named Purgatory Road."

"Pull over, you sonofabitch."

"I'll pull over when you put that disgusting cancer stick back in your pocket."

Charlie glared at him like he glared at Sarah, without the love and lust. He slid the cigarette back into his pocket and put his palm up against the air conditioning duct. "Now, pull this beauty-parlor golf cart over and I'll get the hell out."

Mason spotted a free parking space, yanked at the wheel and braked hard right in front of Perro Salado, a Mexican joint.

He looked over at his old friend. "Fajitas?"

Charlie shrugged and looked at his watch. "Yeah, I guess." He opened the door, plucked the cigarette out of his pocket, and held it up. "I guess I'll meet you inside in five minutes."

CHAPTER FOUR: THE NEXT FEW DAYS

After Mason dropped him off that afternoon, Charlie couldn't stop thinking about his old friend's ridiculous idea, brought up over fajitas, the same one they'd been jawing about since college: the two of them taking a road trip. "Cleveland this summer ... the Rock and Roll Hall of Fame, a game at Progressive Field, maybe a quick scoot over to Canton." Canton was intriguing to Charlie, even though he now thought football was a stupid game. As he had snorted to Mason, "It's really a kind of Coliseum affair where rich suburban fat-asses from Wall Street take their spoiled kids to games for $1,200 a seat, get drunk on the single malts in their flasks, and watch overgrown dark-complexioned men pound the living shit out of each other."

Mason nodded. "Kind of like when white hipsters from the 'burbs went to the Vanguard and the Five Spot to see Mingus, Coltrane, Miles ..." His voice trailed off.

"Us," Charlie had said.

The next morning, in what might have looked like déjà vu to a casual observer, Charlie dropped his usual Tuesday squishy handful of overripe blueberries into the bowl of Special K and, glancing beyond the jar of honey, reached for the sugar and spooned in two overflowing tablespoons. Then a splash of milk. Then another splash. Then a few glugging dribbles to top it off.

And, as before, leaving the milk container on the counter, Charlie slipped the *Globe* under his armpit, picked up the bowl in one hand and a cup of coffee in the other, walked around the island, and sat down at the farm table across from his wife, Sarah. She had her bronze-colored coffee and was reading something on her iPad, the morning sun over the salt marsh making her squint. Charlie automatically listened for BadBreath wheezing and snoring under the table, but of course he wasn't there anymore ... and Charlie closed his eyelids against the rising flood until it seemed to ebb, then opened them and looked across the table at Sarah.

She didn't seem to notice the attention, even after Charlie stared hard at her for a few seconds before picking up his spoon.

Bringing the cereal to his mouth, then letting it sit on his tongue before swallowing, Charlie knew somehow that happiness was still available to him. Still right there in front of him. Just a thin membrane separating him from everything he ever wanted, if only he could step through it. *If only ...*

So, wearing his forlorn mask, he glanced up again at Sarah. As always, it was his way of pleading with her to ask what was troubling him, ask why he was so quiet, ask what she could do to get him out of his funk ... of pleading with her to come up behind him and wrap her arms around him, her chin on his shoulder, her lips at his ear saying, *Tell me, sweet man, what's got you down?* But if Sarah had noticed his gloomy countenance this morning, or had ever noticed it, she had stopped asking a long, long time ago.

Charlie had never learned—if learned is the right word— how to unburden himself, how to talk about the thin membrane of sadness and anger that enveloped him. Especially after Joni. "A grunt," Sarah had said one too many times, "is not an answer to 'What's wrong, honey?'"

Sarah grimaced a decades-old grimace, and, eyes still on the tablet, asked, "What's you got today, Ray?" Ray was her nickname for Charlie, an homage to Man Ray from a long, long time ago, before Woodstock, before Charlie's first

Hasselblad 500CM, before what would turn out to be a career-long gig in the Art Department at Salve Regina, before kids, before grandkids, before cancer, before Joni's accident, before friends' deaths revisited their lives three times, now four times, in one year.

He waited until she looked up. "Nothing much ... the usual crap, a couple of non-productive hours in the studio, a trip to the frame shop, post office. Need to go to Lowe's. You?"

She tilted her head, perhaps wondering when she had tuned out the list, and smiled with some affection. "Meeting Joanna for a Cliff Walk ... shame to pass up such a gorgeous summer day. Then some lunch. House is a mess. Not much." Her eyes back onto the iPad.

Charlie got up, took his bowl, and, without explaining himself, walked out of the kitchen and down the hall to his studio at the back of the house. He had moved his studio from the attic to the old sun room after he gave up on film. Good light. Floor painted kitchen-cabinet green, a soft couch, a long worktable with a paper cutter and messy piles of photographs and colorful mats, windows overlooking the marsh leading out to Sheep Point Cove. Standing next to another farm table which held his oversized computer screen, Charlie slurped up one, two, three spoonfuls of the soggy cereal before sitting.

Next, he booted up the computer and, against his own better judgment, checked his email. The usual crap from PayPal, Orbitz, Chase, the Democratic National Committee; a note from a former student that had started off very pleasantly and ended, as he had suspected it would, with a request for a recommendation; some decent bird pics from his sort-of-friend Solomon, recently retired from the English Department; a grainy cell-phone JPEG of Genevieve's "adorable" grandkids who were in for the week; an invitation from Dharma and Sebastian Bronfels to view photos of their recent trip to Oaxaca on *Snapfish*. "Everyone's a fuckin' photographer these days," he muttered.

"You say something?" Sarah called from the kitchen.

"Just talking to myself," he yelled back, wondering how she'd heard him.

She didn't answer. Or maybe he didn't hear. Anyway, he wasn't listening.

He took a deep breath, in and out through his fleshy nose, then looked up over the screen and out across the green yard, the male bluebird sitting on one birdhouse, his mate perched a few yards away on another, the yellow marsh behind.

***

That night Charlie lay in bed still thinking about a road trip with Mason. He shook his head to get rid of the thought, then stopped when he realized that might wake Sarah. He closed his eyes and started counting lost friends like some people supposedly count sheep. There were the ones who had died, Jim, Jon, Steve, the other Steve, the other Jim. The ones who had disappeared, John, Joe, Barry, Saul. Then there was Stephen Richmond floating behind his eyelids. A sailor. A twenty-year friendship destroyed over the worst of all possible reasons, religion. For some reason that was the loss that stuck in Charlie's craw, and he coughed and flipped from side to side, which finally woke up Sarah.

"What's up, old man?" she whispered through the dark.

"I don't know. I get death," he said, stepping through that membrane as easily as breaking a bubble, as if they were already deep into some conversation. "I get death. You get old, or at least you hope you get old, you get sick, you get hit by a bus, you die."

"Charlie," she said softly, but she stopped there and reached for his hand.

"And moving along, losing touch," he went on as if she had answered him, "I understand that, too. It's a sad life we all lead." They intertwined fingers.

"Who did you lose touch with?"

"Doesn't matter."

"Well," she said, squeezing his hand, "it's not all so sad."

"But religion? Goddamn religion? How does that tear people apart?"

"It's a comfort to a lot of people. Your sister—"

"So is bourbon. So are cigarettes. I bet God weeps at the thought of religion in His name. Tears people apart at the seams. There can only be one god, right?"

She didn't answer, just tightened her grip on his meaty hand. Brought it to her lips and kissed it.

***

A day later Charlie was still thinking about it all—death, God, lost friends, Joni, the trip to Canton—just sitting in his studio, lamp off, slides and prints where he had left them before lunch, staring out at the marsh, when he heard a floorboard squeak. When he turned, his oldest son, Andrew, was standing in the double doorway, flat of his hand up on the jamb. "Hey, Dad ... why don't we hop in that heap of yours and take a drive?"

Charlie was happy to see his grown boy framed in the doorway, no longer a boy, no longer the boy he had once played catch with ... taken fishing ... wrestled in the living room. "That sounds ominous," Charlie grumbled, his upper lip almost approaching a smile. "You in trouble? You need money? You got writer's block? That gorgeous wife of yours kick you out?"

"No, no, no, and no. Not at all, not at all." Both his hands up in the air, Andrew wore a full, toothy smile and below that, the double chin that married men all seem to have acquired by their late thirties. "Nothing like that. I just came to see you. It's been a while."

Charlie frowned. "Your mother put you up to this?"

"Mom? Mom? She's not the boss of me. I'm the captain of my own ship."

"Oh crap, she put you up to this."

Andrew's smile disappeared, replaced by a thin-lipped glare. "Can't you just play along for once in your life, you ornery piece of—" He stopped, standing flat-footed and shoving his hands in his jean pockets, another smile flickering at the edge of his upper lip.

"Apparently not." His own flickering smile

"Well then, yes, Mom asked me to stop by and get your cranky ass out of the house for an hour or two. She said you've been even more of a pain in the ass since BadBreath died. She said—"

"Well, you can tell your mother that I got my own cranky ass out of here, all by myself, no thanks to her. In fact, I just got back from some lousy Thai with that damn fool Mason. We got a weekly ladies lunch thing going."

"Okay then," Andrew said, nodding, "I'm outa here. Do me a favor and tell Mom I did my duty and stopped in—and maybe I'll see you in a couple of weeks at whatever she's planning for Jack's birthday."

As Andrew turned, Charlie mumbled, "Sorry."

Andrew spun back. "What?"

Charlie took a deep breath. And another. "Sorry," he said, louder this time, and stared full faced at the man his oldest child had become.

Andrew's toothy smile reappeared then. "I'm not sure I ever heard you say 'I'm sorry' about anything in the last decade or two. At least since I grew up. You must be mellowing, old man. Is that possible?"

"Oh, I wouldn't say mellowing," Charlie countered quickly. "Maybe I'm just coming down with Zika or something."

Andrew laughed, the same laugh Charlie remembered from the days when Andrew, Dylan, and Joni filled every nook and cranny in the house with the kind of exuberance that generally gets kicked out of kids the moment they step out the door to enter middle school. "Zika just might be the answer to that enormously swelled head you wear." Then he added in a not-unfriendly way, "You are a piece of work."

Charlie liked that. Liked being a piece of work. Offered up that self-satisfied smug look that always drove Sarah nuts. "I'm going to take that as a compliment."

"Y'know," Andrew said, pointing a finger, "I'm gonna finally write something about you one of these days. Lift the veil and tell the truth about the little man behind the curtain, pulling the levers."

Now Charlie was laughing, a full-throated laugh, likely the first one since the kid at Gertie's had yanked one out of him. "Truth?" He mimed Jack Nicholson. "You can't handle the truth! Better stick to your"—air quotes—"YA novels about bullies and fat kids."

And five minutes later, father and son were happily-enough shoulder to shoulder in the battered old Jeep, top down, backing out of the garage with that signature wheeze of the motor.

Andrew looked out at the purple loosestrife grass along the road, the bright blue sky out front. "Where you taking me?" he yelled over the rumble of the engine.

"I want you to meet someone."

"I don't want to meet anyone. And by the way, you need a muffler on this heap."

Charlie took his eyes off the road. "Watch it, kid," he shouted, "you're gonna end up like someone I know, snarling at your wife and kids for no good reason."

"Not a chance. I've spent the better part of the last fifteen years on the couch exorcising that old sonofabitch." Then after a deep nasal inhalation, "And I have to say that it's been particularly difficult the last few years."

Charlie reached over, patted Andrew on the knee, and then reached up to grab the pack of Luckies out of the glove compartment. Flicked up two cigarettes and extended his hand to Andrew, who sneered. "Like I said, a piece of work." And a moment later, as Charlie clamped his lips down on one cigarette and drew it out of the pack, Andrew added, "And don't you dare smoke one of those things in front of my kids."

At the light on Merganser, Charlie found a pack of matches in his breast pocket, lit the cigarette, and blew smoke over his shoulder. And when the light turned green, he drove right past the post office, then the frame shop, then the hospital, signaled a right on Broadway, and headed out of town on 138, roaring past the Lowe's and moving right along as the old Jeep rumbled through Fall River, New Bedford, Wareham.

The two of them were content to not speak, to let the world pass them by without comment. In Sandwich, Charlie pulled into the gravel lot at Gertie's Roadside Rest.

Just as Charlie had figured he would be, the kid was there, sitting astride his bike, leaning on the handlebars, just waiting for something to come along. Mop of dirty blond hair. Freckles. Perked right up when he saw Charlie behind the wheel.

Charlie cut the engine and called out, "Hey, you still just moping around and bugging the customers?"

The boy set his jaw. "I don't bug no customers, mister."

"Take it easy, kid, I was only pulling your leg."

The boy clearly had no idea what leg Charlie was talking about, but he knew he was being made fun of. He looked down at his knees.

"I'm here to introduce you to my son ... and eat one of your mom's lobster rolls." The boy blew out his cheeks in disgust. "And maybe get you some more Ben and Jerry's. Sound good?"

The boy shrugged, a smile snaking across his lips.

"Well, first," thumb pointing to his passenger, "this is my son Andrew. He's got two kids, boy and a girl, the boy almost your age."

The kid seemed unimpressed, but asked, "What school they go to?"

Andrew leaned around his father. "Forgive my father, he lost his manners somewhere in the last century. What's your name?"

The boy glanced at Charlie. Charlie nodded. "Joey," the boy said. He glanced over to the order window. "Joseph."

"Nice to meet you, Joey. We don't live here. We live over in Kingston, Rhode Island, and my kids go to school there."

Another shrug. Another glance toward Charlie.

"I know, I know," Charlie said, "he wears his goddamn pants a little too tight."

Joey frowned. "'Member I said you ain't supposed to take the Lord's name in vain, mister?"

"Right. I forgot. Sorry, kid."

"Sorry?" Andrew piped up just then, unfolding himself from the other side of the Jeep. He shook his head. "That's twice in one day!" He took out his phone and pretended to punch in some numbers. "I gotta call Dylan and let him know the sky is falling."

Charlie glared at his son but said nothing.

Andrew looked around. "Well, who do you want me to meet?"

"Him."

"Him?"

"Him." Left thumb pointing to the boy.

Charlie watched as Andrew's eyes wandered back and forth between his father and the young scruffy boy. "Oh my God, he's not ...?"

Charlie sneered. "Jesus Christ, no! No, no, a thousand times no."

The boy was glowering at both of them now. "I told you, you ain't supposed to take the Lord's name in vain."

"Sorry!" they both said in laughing unison. Andrew had his hands in the air. Charlie repeated himself. "Sorry, kid."

***

An hour later, bellies full of Gertie's lobster rolls and Bud Lites, Joey eating his second small hot-fudge sundae, Charlie and Andrew backed out of the Ben and Jerry's in Sandwich and headed back to Newport. In Wareham, Andrew finally asked, "Why the hell did you want me to meet that kid?"

Charlie shrugged. "I don't know, just something about him ... his transparency ... I think he's a great subject for a series ... your Hardy Boy? My Billy Paine?"

"Who's Billy Paine?"

"Rockwell's first model. Joey could be my last."

"You're kidding." Charlie shrugged again. "Now I'm beginning to think I should stick you in a nursing home."

"That would make some people very happy." Charlie snorted, almost happily, then added, "and, of course, make a whole new group of people very angry."

They both laughed.

And at the next light, Charlie turned to his son. "You better put that nursing-home number on speed dial. I got someone else you need to meet."

***

When they pulled up to the pumps at the Sunoco station back in Newport, Charlie quickly glanced into the convenience store and saw Manny behind the counter. He reached into his breast pocket and took out the pack of Luckies, and with it, a twenty-dollar bill.

He handed Andrew the bill and with a mischievous look said, "That's Manny in there. If I go in, he might shit his pants, so would you introduce yourself to him, tell him we want twenty cranks worth of gas, and then let him know you belong to me?"

"What the hell is this all about?"

"Ah, Andrew, such a worry wort ... I just want you to meet Manny. He's the other one." Charlie dipped two fingers into his breast pocket again to extract another bill. He handed it to his son. "You can get me a pack of Luckies."

"Y'know, I really am getting worried about you."

"Please. I really just want you to meet the kid. I figured you, hotshot writer and all, would be the one who would get it. Anyway, I'll try to explain once I get it all straight in my own head. Please do your pathetic old man a favor, hah?"

Andrew inhaled and exhaled through his nose, his jaw muscles twitching furiously, then nodded and slid out of the Jeep.

Charlie stood behind the pump, hands at his sides, and watched his son enter the shop and go up to the counter. Saw him point out the window toward the Jeep, thought he saw Manny stiffen, and seconds later the pump clicked on. Manny turned to get the pack of Luckies, then Charlie watched the two of them obviously talking, Andrew's head swaying from shoulder to shoulder, Manny pointing to the bays, Andrew reaching across the counter and shaking Manny's hand just before the pump clicked off. Twenty dollars.

By the time Charlie had returned the nozzle, screwed on the gas cap, and glanced one more time into the convenience store, Andrew was back in the Jeep, the new pack of Luckies up on the dash.

"So ...?"

"You wanted me to meet him. I met him. Seems like a nice kid."

"What'd you tell him?"

Andrew clicked the lap belt. "I told him that you are a crazy old coot and that I had the unfortunate luck to have you as a father."

"And what'd he say?"

Andrew glared at him. "He said, 'Please don't let him come in here. There'll be big trouble if my dad sees him.'"

"Was that when he pointed into the bays?"

"Probably. What did you do?"

Charlie shrugged. "I opened my big mouth when ..." He didn't finish.

"Well, let's get the hell away before some angry man comes charging out of there."

For once, Charlie did as he was told without some kind of challenge, and five minutes later father and son were rolling up the driveway at 17 Ledge Road. Charlie cut the engine and held on to the steering wheel while it dieseled into silence. Andrew just sat there waiting until he could wait no more: "So now you gonna tell me what that was all about?"

Charlie turned to look at his son through glassy eyes, seeing through the same watery haze he had seen through after Joni's car went off the bridge in Chapel Hill all those years ago. "Honestly, I don't know. But I know it's important that you met them."

Andrew nodded and patted the old man on the knee.

"I'll let you know as soon as I figure it out."

CHAPTER FIVE: MID-AUGUST

For the forty-second summer in a row, Charlie and Sarah had rented a room at the Nauset Knoll Motor Lodge in East Orleans. The same room, #5. The same third week of August.

They had first discovered this quintessential picture-postcard 1950s Cape Cod cottage court in the late Seventies. And from that time on, they always reserved #5 for the next summer on the morning they checked out. (And #6 too, when the three kids were still young.)

Sarah was sitting on the lawn at one of the round tables overlooking Nauset Beach, the red roof of Liam's hotdog stand sparkling in the sun behind her, the sun on her face. As she confided later to Andrew, wrenching memories of a joyful Joni racing into the water were clouding her eyes.

When Sarah heard Charlie come out of the room, she turned and he couldn't help but see the unhappiness lining her face.

"I've had better receptions at the DMV."

"Don't start. Not today."

"Who's starting? I was just observing that you don't brighten up when I come into view."

"I was thinking of something else."

"What?"

She glared at him, then closed her eyes. A moment later she pushed the wooden chair back and stood up, looking him directly in the eye. "I don't have the energy to do this today. I mean, what the hell is wrong with you?" She turned and headed down the grassy slope to the break in the bushes.

Charlie followed her down the grassy knoll a minute later, lumbering through the opening in the bushes, across the parking lot, past Liam's hot dog stand on the beach, grumbling to himself all the way. And when he caught up to her on the sand, the sun sparkling on the water behind them, it was time to break through the veil. "It's clear you don't love me anymore. If I didn't think Andrew would fall apart, I'd be saying we need to take a break now."

Sarah's ice blue eyes widened. The dam waiting to break. "What are you saying?"

Charlie's slung his jaw open like an old man. Had he finally said it? Did he actually say it out loud?

Sarah didn't wipe away the tears now sliding down her cheeks.

"What do you think I said?" he answered, stalling for time, somewhere in some far-off galaxy in his mind waiting for the declaration of undying love and adoration that he knew would be his, if only ....

Now she wiped her cheeks with a swoop of each shoulder. "I don't know. The waves muffled your words." She sniffed and pointed toward the surf. "That's why I asked."

"Then why are you crying?"

She tilted her head and looked at him like he was a child or a moron. "Because I was thinking about Joni, Charlie. Joni! It's been eighteen years and it's still like it was yesterday. This place just reminds me ..." She didn't finish, and the two of them sat in silence, a warm breeze riffling through her gray hair when she spoke again. "This place always brings back those memories. I did this last year, the first day we were here. I did it the year before. And all the years before that. I sometimes wonder what kind of darkroom you actually live in."

Charlie nodded, chastened, embarrassed, full of the old mourning rising to the surface. His chest rose and fell. Of course, he knew the exact day Joni had died; it might as well have been tattooed on the inside of his eyelids. But he had never put together the pieces on this non-anniversary. He stepped back from the veil. Didn't know what to say. "Maybe we should go someplace else next year. Too many memories here." His voice tailed off in the crashing waves.

Closing her eyes again, Sarah shook her head and muttered, "God, you are such a jackass, Charlie Messina. I need a break from you." She pivoted and started walking up the beach. A few steps away she turned and glared at him. "And don't you follow me."

Twenty yards later she turned again and saw Charlie right where she had left him, standing there flat-footed, hands at his sides, wondering if he was supposed to follow her. "I'll be back later," she called out, the wind and surf muffling her voice. "Do not follow me."

He put his hand behind his ear. "What?" he yelled.

She waved him off, turned, and headed toward North Beach.

***

When Sarah returned a few hours later, Charlie was sitting at one of the round metal tables placed around the green Nauset Knoll lawn. As she appeared, framed in the break of the tall bushes, he dropped his eyes and, feeling naked, pretended to be reading a book.

Approaching the table, she smiled. "I feel better now."

Charlie feigned surprise to see her. "What?" he said, looking up with a warm smile to mirror hers.

Of course, she had to know that he had to be faking it, but she must have decided, as she must have decided a thousand times over forty-five years, to pretend she didn't. "I feel better now," she repeated. Then with another smile, "Isn't it just beautiful today?"

Charlie knew what Sarah was doing, avoiding the next confrontation, but reluctantly decided, as he had reluctantly decided a thousand times over more than four decades, to just go along. The only challenge was to figure out which sentence he needed to respond to … "beautiful day" or "feeling better"? He went with the latter: "Glad you're feeling better." And a moment later, "Sorry I was so damn dense about everything."

Sarah nodded and walked around to a metal chair at a ninety-degree angle from Charlie. "Don't you ever think of her?"

"Every day," he said just above a whisper. "Every goddamn day."

"Yeah?"

He nodded, lowered his chin to his chest when his lower lip started to tremble.

"You don't talk about it."

"If I started to talk about it," he said, staring down into the rusting table top, "I would fall into pieces and nobody would ever be able to put me back together again."

"Oh, you're stronger than that, my Humpty Dumpty. I know."

Charlie pressed his lips together and shook his shaggy gray head. "I don't think so."

"Well, a good cry and a walk on the beach does wonders for me. You should try it sometime."

Charlie nodded, partly in agreement, but mostly so he wouldn't have to talk about Joni anymore. And with that the two of them sat quietly around the white metal table on the green lawn at the Nauset Knoll Motor Lodge, she looking out at the ocean, he holding a book, almost as if they were posing for the new brochure.

After a while, Sarah placed the palms of her hands on the warm table and pushed herself up. "I think I need some wine. Can I get you a glass?"

Charlie glanced over at his wife, still gorgeous after all these years, still able to take his breath away, then looked at his watch. "We haven't eaten lunch yet, Sarah."

"True," she said. "But I need a little courage right now. Then I'll be strong enough for lunch. Can I get you a glass?"

He nodded.

When she returned a few minutes later with the two plastic glasses and an opened bottle of chardonnay, Charlie had nodded off.

He didn't wake up when she put the cup in front of him.

Nor when she poured in two fingers of the cold grape.

Nor when she reached over and tousled his hair. "Courage, my sweet man."

He didn't move.

"Charlie?"

PART II

"I sit with Shakespeare and he winces not. Across the color-line I move arm in arm with Balzac and Dumas, where smiling men and welcoming women glide in gilded halls. From out the caves of the evening that swing between the strong-limbed earth and the tracery of the stars, I summon Aristotle and Aurelius ... and they come all graciously with no scorn nor condescension. So, wed with Truth, I dwell above the Veil."

— W.E.B. Du Bois, *The Souls of Black Folk*

CHAPTER SIX (OR ONE): AUGUST 18

He opens his eyes and finds himself peering out from behind a thin veil. Not the invisible veil that has separated him from the rest of the world, the one he knows like a shadow twin. Not a wedding veil. More like a thin, lacy curtain across some stage. He can make out shapes, can hear voices. He even knows he can step through the opaque curtain, should step through it, into the light; the audience waits, but he can't move, legs heavy as if they were stuck in river muck or maybe cement, atrophied arms too weak to even reach for the break in the veil, to pull it apart, to step onto the stage, into the light, and tell them he is here, that he can hear them.

He remembers changing babies. Cloth diapers. Lifting those cherubic feet with three fingers. Holding their bottoms up in the air. Wiping the sweet disgusting shit off their soft skin. All those folds! Folding the wet diaper then and dropping it on the floor. Cleaning between all the folds. Folds everywhere, folds everywhere, legs up in the air, those naked babies giggling, making him giggle, airing out on the changing table. The dirty diaper on the tile floor. Picking it up between thumb and forefinger, holding the diaper at the cleanest corner over the toilet bowl and letting it unravel, sweet shit tumbling into the water. Then, yes, dunking the shitty diaper into the water, dunking it again, and again, and again until the water was brown and the diaper nothing but stains. And then the deep breath, the daily, daily, daily deep breath, knowing that there was no way to avoid getting shit on his hands, quickly stepping through that veil, grabbing the waterlogged, shitty diaper in both hands, wringing it, wringing it again and again until there was no more brown water dripping into the toilet. Turning and opening the diaper pail and dropping it in.

***

Now he hears a younger male voice. A doctor? Does he see or just imagine the distinctive top of a Montblanc pen sticking out of the man's white coat and a head shaved bald? He hears the doctor, if he is a doctor, saying, "It's AV nodal reentrant tachycardia." Then silence. A sigh. "That's a rapid heart rate due to more than one pathway through the AV node."

When there is no response (someone nodding? Sarah?), the voice goes on: "It's a pretty common arrhythmia. We treated him with Adenosine, Diltiazem, and digitalis, and so far he has responded quite well."

Now Charlie is sure it is Sarah behind the veil. He is sure he sees her nod. That she understands. "I'm going to suggest you contact your husband's cardiologist in Newport as soon as you get him home." Another nod? "I'm sure he'll prescribe calcium channel blockers and probably some long-acting beta-blockers—maybe digitalis. In any case, I'm going to have your husband transferred downstairs this afternoon to a room in the Stepdown unit. And I don't see any reason why you shouldn't be able to take him home tomorrow."

Through the gauze Charlie sees Sarah extend her hand to shake the doctor's hand, but the doctor is already stepping around her, his hand touching her shoulder, his soft brown loafers clip-clopping away down the quiet hall, bald head gleaming from the ceiling lights. And just before he turns the corner, "Of course, he needs to stop smoking."

Now Charlie imagines the scowl that spreads across Sarah's lined face as she mutters, "Not going to happen."

***

62

An hour later, Charlie is sleeping in Room 437 of the step-down unit, Sarah sitting in a straight-backed chair beside the bed, Andrew and his wife Cecilia standing silently behind her, Dylan sitting on the AC/heating unit, staring out the window.

Sarah has been holding Charlie's hand since they wheeled him in here. She leans down and presses her cheek to the back of his hand, then glances over her shoulder to Andrew. "He's pretty drugged up right now. I'm going to get a cup of coffee and sit outside for a while." She turns her head around the other way. "One of you sit here in case he wakes up."

To her surprise it is Dylan, forty-one, who walks over and slides into her chair. Dylan, with dreads and a full sleeve of richly-colored tattoos from bicep to wrist. Dylan, who plays bass guitar in a band he named for BadBreath long before the dog died. Dylan, who dropped out of Harvard a month before he was supposed to graduate and disappeared in London. Dylan, who hasn't spoken to his father since their big row over Christmas about something completely unrelated to their lives—the politics of the West Bank.

Dylan reaches through the rail, takes his father's thick mitt, and cups it between both of his four-ringed hands. Andrew comes up behind him and lays both of his hands on his brother's shoulders, squeezes and bends over to kiss Dylan on the top of his head. Then Cecilia, one hand on Andrew's back, leans around and kisses Dylan on the cheek.

Dylan doesn't turn but shakes his head. "I'm just thinking about the three of us lobstering up on Monhegan that fall ..."

Which is when Charlie seems to awaken—or at least opens his eyes briefly and shudders at something. Then closes them tight like a child might do upon seeing a monster or a ghost, quickly sinking back into what looks like a deep sleep. An agitated sleep. An incoherent mumbling sleep. Now he is fumbling with Dylan's fingers, turning one ring, then the other, then another, growing more and more agitated as he moves, eyes clamped shut, through each of the remaining five rings, then slapping them away.

Dylan looks back over his shoulder. "What the hell does the old bugger want?"

Andrew shakes his head. "I don't know. Let me sit there for a minute. See if that makes a difference."

It doesn't. Charlie blindly fumbles with Andrew's wedding ring, twists it around and around, and then, just like he had done with Dylan, slaps the hand away. Then slaps the mattress once, twice, three times before Cecilia nudges Andrew with her hip and slides in next to him.

She takes his hand in her soft palms as if she were praying. She whispers, "Charlie, it's me, Cecilia, I'm here for you. I'm so glad you're going to be okay."

She starts to cry. "You scared the living hell out of me."

On any given day, funny, gorgeous, blond, snarky Cecilia, who Charlie occasionally thinks looks like she had just walked off a shoot with Bill Cunningham, is the only one in the family who seems to enjoy him without reservation. And he is unabashedly smitten with her. Always has been. Especially since Joni died. As Andrew says, "Everything is A.J. in this family."

And for a minute or two Charlie seems to calm down. His eyes are closed but no longer clamped shut. He has stopped mumbling and seems to sink into the mattress. But when his fingertips touch Cecilia's engagement ring, and turn it once, then twice, he starts mumbling again, almost as if he were speaking in tongues, moving from one finger to the next, returning to her diamond, then her wedding band, turning it, turning it, then slapping both hands away, the flat of his hand slapping the mattress once, twice, three times.

"Andrew, go get your mother," Cecilia says. "He wants her."

Andrew looks at his wife like she is daft. "Did he say something to you that I didn't hear?"

"Go," she says. And when he doesn't move, she points toward the door and repeats, "Go!" just like she might to their two kids.

And five minutes later, Charlie still mumbling through some drug-induced nightmare, mother and son appear in the doorway, Andrew's arm around Sarah's shoulder. He steps back and allows her to walk into the room first. Her face is ghostly.

Cecilia stands and reaches for her mother-in-law's hand. "I guess Andrew told you."

Teary-eyed, Sarah takes Cecilia's hand and says, "He just told me I needed to come up. I thought—" She looks at her husband mumbling and grumbling—and breathing—and the color begins to return to her cheeks.

"He seemed to be searching for you, your hand," Cecilia offers. "He batted away Dylan's hand, then Andrew's, then mine." She laughs an anxious laugh and pulls out the chair.

Sarah takes her seat next to the hospital bed and cups Charlie's hand in hers. And when he finds her emerald-cut diamond ring—the one that had belonged to his mother—he calms down. Turns it around and around. Stops mumbling. His forehead grows smooth again.

"Amazing," Cecilia says and glances at her husband, tears in her eyes.

"Hard guy to figure out," Dylan says just above a whisper from over by the AC unit. His cheeks are wet.

"Not so hard," Cecilia says.

Now Andrew's lower lip is quivering. "I'll tell you about my trip to the Cape with him sometime. Hard to figure is only the tip of the iceberg sinking the battleship we call Dad."

Which is when Charlie, eyes still closed, slips his hand out of Sarah's grasp and lays his palm on her knee, caressing it, caressing it, then moving up along the outside of her thigh.

"Oh my God," Andrew says, scowling, "the old letch is trying to grab a piece while he's unconscious."

Cecilia laughs and slaps him on the shoulder. "It's sweet."

Sarah ignores both of them and pulls the chair as close to the rail as it goes, Charlie's hand bulged at her hip. "We're gonna be okay. We're gonna be okay."

Charlie's heavy-lidded eyes open partway. Moments later his lips seem to smile and he opens his mouth as if to say something, but what comes out is so hushed, Sarah can't make it out.

"What are you saying, Ray?" she whispers, and the others, hearing her question, lean in behind her.

He opens his mouth once more, but all that comes out are more whispery breath sounds, the words drowned out by the hum of hospital machines.

"What'd he say?" asks Dylan.

Sarah shakes her head and shrugs.

"And what did you call him? Ray?"

Sarah turns to her oldest with a little-girl smirk he has only witnessed a few times. "'Nother time, Dylan. Another time." She is still smiling when she asks Charlie again what he is saying, but this time she leans over close enough to feel his warm breath on her ear.

"I saw St. Augustine," he whispers.

She leans back and scowls. "You did not see St. Augustine, you old goat. This is a bad time to be making jokes. You don't even believe—"

"He saw St. Augustine?" Cecilia asks, breaking the drop-jaw silence all around.

Sarah, craning her head around, says, "He's incorrigible. A few weeks ago, he ruined an absolutely pleasant dinner party with some new friends when he refused the host's request to hold hands and silently—silently! —give thanks to God for the meal and 'good friends' to share it."

"What'd he do?" Dylan asks from behind her, a toothy smile brightening his face.

Sarah's face is stony. "Your father stood up and said something like, 'If I give your damn God thanks for all this, we'd all have to acknowledge that while he is indulging us, he is actually choosing to starve millions and millions of others around this heartless planet. And frankly I don't think you want to believe any god is capable of such cruelty.' Then he said something like, 'I'm doing you all a favor.'"

Cecilia covers her laugh with her palm. "I love that. So what did the host say?"

Sarah finally cracks a smile. "She stiffened and said they always give thanks before eating."

"So ...?"

"Charlie walked out."

"And what did you do?"

Sarah shakes her head. "What could I do? I told them he was on a new medication—and apologized—and left."

They are all chortling now. Except Andrew. Andrew throws his hands up in the air and turns away. "I don't get it. And St. Augustine? Why the hell not Jesus himself?"

With another laugh Dylan blurts out, "Jesus would be too cliché for our father who art not in heaven. He really is a piece of work."

Sarah hushes the two men like they are still her boys, and then leans over and presses her lips to Charlie's ear. "Did you say that you saw St. Augustine? I'm not sure I heard right."

He nods, eyes still closed. then whispers hoarsely, "Alive as you or me."

In the silence that follows, Dylan turns to his mother. "That's a line from Dylan's "I Dreamed I Saw St. Augustine." He really is a piece of work." He is not trying to be funny.

CHAPTER SEVEN (OR TWO): LATER AUGUST

A week later, Dylan is sitting on a wooden chair painted red in the studio, while outside bright sun glints off the marsh weeds shimmering after a sun shower.

Charlie swivels around on the metal stool—and answers an entirely different question than the one he was asked: "I wasn't joking. I saw him."

"Who?"

"I saw St. Augustine."

Dylan stares wide-eyed, speechless, a thin grin holding back what Charlie thinks might let out the same kind of fearful wail he used to do when he was a small child. "That's not what I asked you. I asked—"

"I know. But I did. I did. No joke, Dylan. And please ... sotto voce ...," he adds, pointing back toward the kitchen.

"How did you know it was him?" Dylan whispers.

"I just knew. And what's more"—he looks over Dylan's shoulder to make sure Sarah is not behind him—"Joni was standing right next to him."

"Joni?"

"Shhh. I don't want your mom to know. It'll just make her upset, and she's been through a lot lately."

Dylan nods, a scowl now erupting at the corner of his lips. "You're jerking me around."

"No. And don't you dare tell Andrew. He'll have me put away. I sometimes think that if it wasn't for the beautiful Cecilia blocking his path, Andrew—with your mother's approval—would have signed me into that fucking St. Claire's warehouse for the senile years ago." Charlie bends over then, elbows pressed onto his thighs, turns his head. "Anyway, she looked good. Happy. Exactly like she was that summer," adding, "before, you know. She was twenty. She'll always be twenty."

"I don't know what to say, Dad."

Charlie shrugs and reaches over with a grunt for his son's knee. Squeezes it. "I don't either."

Dylan's eyes are cloudy. "So ... what did Joni say?"

"She didn't say anything. She just smiled at me. Sweetly. I mean, really sweetly, like I'd sometimes see her when she'd be sitting on the deck and listening to you play your guitar all alone in the backyard." His hand is still on Dylan's knee.

"So ...," Dylan whispers again, eyes flooding, pausing, then glancing through the window at the sparkling green yard, "so, what, um, did St. Augustine say to you?"

"He didn't say anything. Mom's right, I don't even believe in God. In fact, it didn't seem like he even noticed me. Maybe it wasn't St. Augustine, just some drugged-out bum in robes. Anyway, I thought he was St. Augustine—and he was just standing there right next to Joni. I am sure it was her. Then some dog came up to them."

"Dog? BadBreath? He's dead, too, Dad."

"They're all dead, Dylan. All three—Augustine, Joni, the Breath. This dog was nothing like the Breath, except he was fat."

"So just a random dog?"

"Yeah, you know, kind of an overweight blockheaded mutt, black, thick tail wagging. Like an obese lab. Do you remember Dizzy Gillespie, the black lab we had when you were little?"

Dylan nods.

"Like him, but different. Fat. And the three of them were standing in line at a lobster-roll stand on the Cape."

"I don't know what to say, Dad. Sounds a little far out to me."

"I'm not saying it isn't, but I'm not making it up—and as far as I can tell, I'm not crazy."

"So ...," Dylan continues to whisper, "what do you think it means?" He looks away then, toward the marsh.

Charlie takes his hand off Dylan's knee and sits up straight. "You see something?"

A brisk shake and then a clipped "No," but Charlie knows Dylan did.

"Well, I don't know what it means. It was kind of hazy, like I was looking through a gauzy veil."

Dylan nods.

"I don't think I've ever told you," he says, stepping through another membrane of sorts, "that I've lived my whole life behind some kind of veil. In fact, I feel like—right now, right here"—he presses his index finger into his thigh—"I feel like in telling you this, right now, it feels like maybe I have just walked through another gauzy layer. And I must say that the clarity of the images I'm just beginning to see is stunning. I wish I could share it with you."

Dylan continues nodding like some bobblehead doll, the thin, fixed smile back on his pale, bearded face.

"And just for the record, I don't think that's the end of the veils." Charlie turns to check the doorway—no one there—and back to Dylan, who is still staring out at the marsh. "Y'know, I don't think I ever told you—or Andrew; pretty sure I spoke about this to Joni once, though. I was born with a caul."

Dylan glances back at his father, confusion written all over his face. "I'm sorry, I have no earthly idea what you're talking about."

"Doesn't matter," Charlie starts to say, still whispering, but he can't stop himself from going on. "It's a kind of thin membrane that covers some babies' heads when they're born.

In medieval times the appearance of a caul on a newborn baby was seen as a sign of good luck. My mother—"

"So?"

"My mother thought it made me special, thought I was special in God's eyes, but I think it just kept me from getting close to anyone."

Moments later, after the air in the studio has gone still, the two of them breathless, Charlie murmurs, "And then, wouldn't you know it, the damn mutt showed up at the back door yesterday!"

Turning his head from side to side, then quickly glancing back toward the kitchen, Dylan whispers, "Dog? Where's the dog?"

"I guess you can't see it."

"I can't see it."

"Right. You can't see it. But I'm not crazy, son. I'm just finding out that once you step through a veil, you can see things that were hidden in all those gauzy layers that keep us cocooned. Things that were always there but just never noticed. You know what I mean?"

"Yeah. No. I guess." Dylan scans the studio and stares out through the window into the marsh. "You do know I can't see a dog."

"Yes, Dylan."

"So where is it?"

"Right here," Charlie says, pointing to the side of his shoe. "And now you're looking at me like you're really afraid I'm crazy."

Dylan's flat smile grows toothy. "Well, you're right, I am definitely afraid that you're crazy. Batshit loony tunes, if you really want to know." He presses his lips together, then adds, "But I have to say that I almost kind of like it. After the last how many years? Batshit loony tunes would be a relief."

***

A week later Charlie is watching Dylan do sound checks for the BadBreath gig at the Calvin in Northampton, Massachusetts, when Dylan first notices his father in front of the stage, down on one knee, Nikon pressed to his forehead.

"Dad?"

"Hi, son. Just keep doing what you're doing."

"I'm doing a sound check. What're you doing? What the hell are you doing here? Does Mom know you're here? Aren't you supposed to be taking it easy for a while?"

"Well, working backwards. I'm done taking it easy ... and no, I'm not gonna lie, Mom thinks I'm off on a yoga retreat."

"She does not."

"Well," Charlie grins, "something like that. A nature photography weekend."

"Then, what the hell are you doing here?"

"I'm documenting your tour." He presses the button and holds it—click, click, click, click. "Not the usual kind of rock and roll shit that passes for art," he adds without being asked. "I have just come to see what you're doing. What you've been doing all these years. And I'm documenting it. Making up for some lost time." He presses his palm to the floor and, with a grunt, stands.

Dylan places his hand over the mic. "Did we talk about this?"

"No. I spoke to Joni's dog, if it's Joni's dog. Name's Dumbass ...," he says as he lowers the camera and raises his eyebrows. "Seemed like a good idea, so here I am."

"Dumbass? Is that the name of the dog or are you reverting to form and calling me an idiot?"

"No! That's the name of the dog."

Looking all around to see who is privy to this bizarre conversation, Dylan asks, "Does he speak to you?"

"Don't be an idiot, Dylan. Of course, he doesn't speak to me. He's a dog. It's all in the gesture. Everything is in the gesture. The authentic gesture. When no one is looking."

Speechless, Dylan shrugs, just as he had done a week before in the studio. But now he doesn't seem quite as charmed by his newly strange old man as he had been back in Newport.

"Step through the veil and you come to understand words don't mean a thing," Charlie goes on. "That's why I'm documenting your tour—but not the performance part of it, all those ridiculous faces narcissistic musicians like to make and all those know-nothing photographers love to snap. I'm documenting the real stuff, this." His hand sweeps around the empty space. "You. Dylan. You're an artist."

"I don't know what to say."

"Y'know, you say that a lot."

"Well, there's a lot going on, and we haven't spoken in a long time. And frankly, you're talking about dogs that aren't there."

"Dogs you can't see."

"Right. Dogs I can't see."

"Good. We'll save that for another time. You do your work. I'll take some photographs—and then after the show you and me and Mason"—he jams his thumb toward the back of the room, and Mason waves from the shadows— "we'll talk some more."

"Is that Mason?"

"You do see him, right?"

"I do. What the hell is he doing here?"

"He's a musician."

"Yeah, right, so what?"

"Turns out that he's a fan of BadBreath. Told me a few weeks ago over lunch at some Mexican joint in Newport. I never knew that. But that's not why he's here."

Dylan scans the dark theater again. His bandmates and their one official roadie look like they are playing a game of freeze tag, each one frozen in mid-action, watching the drama going on at the lip of the stage, leaning in to try to hear the conversation between the old man and their lead guitar. Then Dylan glances back. "Okay, I'll bite."

"While I was still in the hospital, I began to realize what you've really been doing with your music all these years. And by the time I got home and leached all those goddamn drugs out of my system, I knew for certain—"He stops abruptly then and glares into Dylan's gleaming eyes. "Well, I knew for certain that Joni was right back then"—Dylan raises his eyebrows—"that you weren't just another privileged, over-educated, longhaired Newport jerkoff trying to get laid."

"Well, thank you very much." Dylan snorts, now gesturing with both hands for his friends onstage behind him to bug off. "Your support has always been so comforting."

"Oh, Christ, you know what I mean. Stupid as it was, I understood why you left Harvard. I understand. You're an artist. The real deal." Charlie reaches for the pack of Luckies in his breast pocket and, assured it is there, says, "It's damn hard with a foot in two worlds. I gotta stop talking like I'm still behind the veil."

"What?"

"Oh nothing, the old me is just getting acclimated to the new me. Or is it just another me? Oh, forget it." He lifts the camera clickclickclick.

Dylan inhales through his nose and then empties his lungs through his dry mouth. "So ... what the hell is Mason doing here if he didn't come to hear the band play?"

"He's officially my consultant on this project. He's a royal pain in the ass as you know, but he's also a true believer, a real musician ... at least somewhere in his lecherous soul. And, frankly, he's the one, the only one I trust to cue me when there's something I should document. I'm an idiot when it comes to all this—and he's going to let me know when the moment is coming around."

Dylan scrunches his lips together. "So … what the hell am I supposed to do?" His free hand, fingers strumming, flies up in the air.

"Nothing." Charlie glances down then and swats at the air around his knees. "Stop it!" Then he looks up at his boy. "Not you, Dylan. And no, you don't have to do anything. I'll just be around the edges, taking pictures, trying to stay out of your way."

"Tonight?"

"Yeah, of course tonight. Then next week at Lupo's in Providence. Then"—he pulls a card out of his breast pocket—"your midweek gig at Baxter's Boathouse in Hyannis. And finally that big-deal thing you got going at the Bridgeton Music Hall."

"Brighton."

"Okay, Brighton. Can't read my own handwriting. Anyway, don't look so damn horrified. I'm not following you to England."

***

During the sold-out show, Charlie mostly keeps to himself in the shadows, occasionally lifting the camera when Mason points to Dylan fine-tuning an amp or biting a fingernail or gesturing with his eyes toward the drummer. The real work for Charlie, though, comes after the show, after the last encore, after the last patron has left the theater, after someone passes around a case of Coronas—clickclickclick—and the stage is buzzing with wires being looped and guitars and drums being packed away, when the staged smiles disappear and are replaced by the easy talk among people for whom talking is unnecessary, Mason with his lanky arm around Dylan, the scraggly bass-guitar guy pausing to eavesdrop on what they are saying or not saying. Clickclickclick. Clickclickclick. Clickclickclick.

Charlie is already weary beyond weary when Dylan comes over and says, "We're headed over to the Iron Horse for a couple of shots and maybe one more unscheduled set." Dylan mimes some air quotes, and Charlie looks confused. "James McMurtry. He's over there tonight working solo. You don't know him?"

Mason, who also looks tired, nods and offers a thumbs-up.

"So ... you want to join us?"

"Well, no. But this is apparently what I signed on for—and you're leaving soon—so lead the way. I guess I'm in for the ride."

CHAPTER EIGHT (OR THREE): EARLY SEPTEMBER

"Y'know, Dylan thinks I'm crazy." Charlie is talking to the pine floor just beyond his right sneaker. "And not because I told him I saw St. Augustine at the lobster-roll joint. Or because Joni was standing right there next to him. It's because of you."

Checking the doorway before reaching down and mussing the dog's shaggy head, its ears flipping around so charmingly, Charlie adds, "I get Jesus, even if I don't totally get the cross. And although I wish it weren't so, I get Joni. I get Joni standing there. I've been feeling her around me for ... oh Christ, I ..." His voice trails off.

He sits still for a few moments, not breathing, not moving, thoughtless as the wind moving through the reeds. Then he shakes the silence out of his head. "But I don't get where you come into all this. Why you were there in the first place—and why the hell you showed up here? I just don't get it. Plus, with you around and humping my leg, there's no way that all of 'em are not gonna think I'm totally nuts."

The dog spins and spins and spins and finally lies down. "Maybe I am crazy. Maybe I didn't see anything. Maybe you should get your dumb ass outa here."

The dog stands and stretches. Yawns. Tongue pointing. Starts walking toward the door. "Hey, don't be like that!" Then Charlie lowers his voice: "Don't leave." And even lower, a mumble, "Truth is I sort of like having you around. Lets me know what layer I'm in. Anyway, just do me a favor and stick around until I figure out what you're doing here. Please."

Now he is talking out of the side of his mouth: "I think I'm going to officially register your name with the AKC as Dumbass. Okay? I mean it in the nicest possible way. And about that humping my leg thing ... just in case it was you, it's goddamn bad manners and it makes me look like I'm some kind of doddering old spastic. Just stop it. You're too old anyway."

The dog lifts his eyelids and closes them again.

"Good! I think we understand each other."

A moment later the dog has disappeared, not having walked the conventional way through the doorway and down the hall to go wherever he might be going. No. As Charlie instantly understands—or thinks he understands—the hound simply stepped through a veil without explanation. This is no talking dog.

Charlie returns to the series he is developing on Dylan, his contact sheets spread around the worktable, jeweler's glass in his eye, two manila folders lying where they'd been for weeks. One contains several contact sheets from his two visits to the kid Joey on the Cape; the other just has one sheet from that wild afternoon with Manny and his old man Raul at the Sunoco. Charlie keeps speaking to the dog, even though the dog isn't there: "I know this is all of a piece ... I just don't know what the hell the piece is."

He glances down at his feet again, then over at the door. Nothing. No one. No dog. And with that, he experiences a powerful craving for a cigarette. Feels in his breast pocket for the pack—just shy of full—and, pressing down with both palms on the worktable, hoists himself up and lumbers to the open doorway, down the hall, and into the kitchen, where Sarah is sitting, eating an avocado drizzled with balsamic vinegar while reading something on her iPad.

"You're home!"

She doesn't look up. "I live here."

"I just thought you were out at your book group ... or what is today? Thursday? Your clay class."

"Ceramics. Canceled. Jean-Claude is sick."

"I'll bet you that phony bastard is from Queens—and his name is Irving or Seymour Lipschutz."

"Nice, Charlie. Very nice." She turns to find him standing at the kitchen door. "First, he's a very nice man ... and second, he grew up in Marseilles ... and third, he's a world-class potter. And do I detect some latent anti-Semitism in your choice of names? Y'know, you could be a lot kinder."

He shrugs, chastised. "I could be."

"And besides, I thought you were a changed man."

All the air goes out of his lungs then. He closes his eyes. Breathes in. Breathes out with a whoosh. "You're right. You're absolutely right. Of course, you're right. I'm sorry. I am a cranky sonofabitch ... but not all the way through. As I was telling Dylan the other day, sometimes it's confusing having a foot in two worlds."

She sneers. "And which worlds would that be?"

"The layers. The ones I was talking about the other day, each one separated by a thin veil. And I'm beginning to think there are lots of layers, not just two."

Sarah lifts the spoon with a chunk of avocado oily with balsamic dressing. "Want a bite?"

He shakes his head, points to the cigarette.

"So, you're still thinking that you walked through some kind of veil? That's when you saw St. Augustine?"

"Yes."

"And Joni?" Now Sarah looks halfway between smirking and crying.

He doesn't know whether he is being chided or if she actually wants to discuss his new theory of parallel time separated by thin, invisible veils. "I guess I do," he says, knowing that it is no guess at all.

Sarah rocks her head from side to side and offers a thin but sweet smile. "Pretty damn crazy, my love." She seems lost in thought then. "But not the craziest thing I ever heard. I—"

His knee buckles. He wonders if the dog nosed him in the back of his leg. Yes? No? "I gotta go," he says, thumb pointing out the door.

Sarah doesn't look up. "Have fun," she says as if she were talking to a child.

And by the time he makes it over to the garage, Dumbass is waiting in the passenger seat. Looks over at him and licks his nose.

"So what? Are you saying you want to go to the Cape?"

Dumbass stretches out his leg, bends his head, and with a snort begins licking his balls.

"You're not fixed?"

No response.

"Turns out my politically-correct son Andrew got himself fixed a couple of years ago. Even after I told him he'd be a moron for doing it. Told him straight out that you never know what's around the next corner, what's going to happen when you step through the next veil. There's always a veil, you know. He had no idea what I was talking about."

Reaching around the steering wheel, Charlie shoves the key into the ignition. At the sound of combustion, the dog hunkers down on the ripped seat, snout planted on his outstretched paws. "And, by the way, don't ever nose me in the back of the knee again. I'm an old man ... I could fall and do some real damage."

Jamming the shifter into reverse, Charlie eases up on the clutch and backs out of the garage onto Ledge Road, the whine of the engine as comforting as ever. "In fact, don't touch me at all. I'll just pet you whenever the mood strikes." He reaches over then and shakes the dog's ears. "Hey, don't be insulted. I like you, and, just for the record, I'm the real dumbass."

Ass out on Ledge Road, Charlie laughs out loud before singing a line from "I Am The Walrus."

Dumbass closes his eyes.

***

A few days later Charlie is back in his studio looking down at his feet, wondering where the dog has gone this time.

Eventually he returns to the series he seems to be developing on Joey and Manny, contact sheets spread around the worktable, jeweler's glass in his eye, all those visits to the Cape; the ones at the Sunoco, including that wild, tragic afternoon with Manny's old man, Raul. Next Charlie picks up some more recent photos of his grandson Jack—and granddaughter Diane. And then, of course, all the shots of Dylan at the Calvin. It's all feeling like some kind of déjà vu.

And then talking to the dog, even though the dog isn't there, Charlie says, "I know this is all of a piece ... even the series on Dylan, I just don't know what the hell the piece is— or how the pieces are related to each other. I don't know what I'm doing, dog." He reaches down for Dumbass's block head, but of course there is just air. Then, drawing in a deep breath through his words: "It is what it is."

A knock on the door frame to the studio startles him. Dylan. Standing like da Vinci's *Vitruvian Man*, clothed of course but feet spread and both hands extended, each pressed into the opposite door jamb.

"Hey." Dylan smirks at his own yet-to-be-spoken joke. Then he tilts his head like he's going to say something he knows that Charlie won't like.

"Yeah, hey ... and what tidings of comfort and joy you bringing for me?"

"Got some news, big news, good news," Dylan says and pauses, perhaps waiting for Charlie to ask him to go on.

"Go on," Charlie says, frankly more relieved than anxious to hear of some triumph rather than another whine. "Shoot."

"Well"—another smile awkwardly stifling a laugh—"BadBreath just got a major gig ... long story short, but there was a late cancellation and now we're headlining at the October BuckyFest out in Madison, Wisconsin, and—"

"BuckyFest? What in the hell is a Buckyfest? An orthodontist convention?"

"Jesus Christ, Charlie, just fuckin' listen—"

"Don't call me Charlie," he grumbles, but then quickly flashes a smile that he feels is perilously close to exploding into a wail. "Sorry." Both men hold their breaths. Then, "I am officially stopping being a Class A pain in the ass right now. So, tell me ..."

Dylan raises his eyebrows in stunned disbelief. "Okay. I'll take you at your word. Anyway, not sure what's going on, but it's a big-time concert series—like, hmmmm, Saratoga?" He pauses then, but Charlie doesn't seem to understand. "Bonnarroo?" A shrug. "Burning Man?" Another shrug. "Okay ... the Newport Folk Festival?"

"Yup. Okay. Gotcha. So?"

"Well, like I said, this is a big deal—a really big deal for the band—and we were wondering, I was wondering, if you—and maybe you and Mason—want to go along and document the whole thing? We all liked what you did up at the Calvin and ..." He doesn't finish.

Charlie feels himself flush and is just about to stand and stride over to give his son a big hug of gratitude when Dylan holds up his hand. "Just for the record, no matter how many veils"—he flashes some air quotes—"you supposedly step through, you are always going to be a Class A pain in my ass." He smiles.

And Charlie leans back on the stool. "Touché ... and for whatever it's worth, right back at ya."

Chapter Nine (or Four): Late October

Charlie is leaning back in a metal chair on the lakeside terrace of the Rathskeller at the University of Wisconsin. He is soaking in the sun and privately reliving the standing ovation BadBreath had received the night before at the Buckyfest when he feels a buzz in the pocket of his khakis. He shifts around, digs deep, pulls out his cell phone, and glances at the screen, then at Mason slurping some coffee (and shamelessly ogling a coed walking by). Then he looks down at the dog under the table, snout on his sneaker.

"Sara, Smile!" he croaks into the phone, referencing the Hall and Oates tune. But before she has a chance to groan, he says, "Dylan was fabulous last night. I'm—"

"It's me, Dad," Andrew interrupts on the other end. "I'm at the house ... Mom ..." This is followed by deep gasps like he's hyperventilating.

Charlie tells him to slow down, then listens without taking another breath to a deluge of words, but only hears the staggering punch-in-the-gut line.

Twenty hours and seven states later, Mason drops Charlie off at the Cape Cod house on Ledge Road. It is 7 a.m. Andrew's car is in the driveway. So is Dumbass.

As soon as Charlie unfolds himself from the cramped Cabriolet, now stinking of the residue of McDonald's meals and Charlie's smoky jacket, he sees his middle-aged son striding out of the kitchen door, arms wide open, unshaven cheeks blotchy with tears. Andrew wraps his arms around his slumping father, who nearly falls over, who over a thousand miles has had nearly a full day to contemplate the next veil he has no choice but to step through, the loneliness unto death that awaits him, the remorse that has already begun to haunt him. This sorrow he knows will haunt him all through the rest of his days. And nights.

When Charlie regains his balance, he stands stock still, allowing the sobbing Andrew to hold him, to hold him up, when all he wants to do is fall to the pavement and never ever get up again. "She's gone, Dad!" Andrew cries as if it is news. "She's gone!"

***

Cecilia is in the kitchen when Charlie walks in. She has been preparing drinks and plates for their friends who will be stopping by. She dries her hands on a towel. Her eyes pooling, she stands on her tiptoes and wraps her arms around Charlie's warm, thick neck. "Oh, Charlie ..."

Then she whispers in his ear that the kids are at school and they'd be around later.

Charlie nods and walks around her, down the hall and into his studio. He sits heavily on the stool in front of his worktable and stares out at the marsh. Andrew soon follows him in, sits on the small floral couch Sarah had set up in there so Charlie could read in the late afternoons, the sun glistening through the windows. "Can I get you anything?"

Charlie shakes his head.

"I guess we need to talk about arrangements," he says a minute or two later, but Charlie can't talk, just raises his hand, shakes it, then drops it down past his knee where the dog is waiting for it.

***

Dylan flies into Hartford that afternoon. Andrew picks him up, and the two brothers drive straight home to find Charlie still in his studio, sorting through thousands of photographs of Sarah, placing them in piles year by year, from the months

85

before they were married to the day, a week before, that Charlie and Mason (and Dumbass) had taken off for Dylan's gig at the Buckyfest.

Charlie hears a knock and looks around to find his bereft sons in the studio doorway, hands at their sides like little boys. Eyes bloodied and narrowed, he shakes his head and lets his chin fall to his chest. Moments later both sons are at his sides, each with one hand on his arm, the other on his back, leaning over and laying their cheeks on his shoulders, weeping.

Crushed beneath their shared sobs, Charlie reaches blindly under the table for Dumbass and finds his floppy ears, his wet nose. The only creature in the house not in mourning. And perhaps because of that simple fact, Dumbass is the only comfort Charlie can find over the next week, a hand on the dog's shoulder, on his block head, floppy ears caressed between thumb and forefinger, one day stumbling into the next with what seems like an endless mourners' parade of hugs and tears and "I'm sorry"s and "She was the most wonderful"s and "Let me know"s. The refrigerator is stuffed with casseroles, the sideboards and windowsills with flowers, the blinking phone with messages.

The bed empty.

"I can't call you Dumbass anymore," Charlie says one night, staring up at the ceiling from his side of the king-size bed, parting another veil. The dog is on the floor next to him. "Don't ask me why; I just can't. And don't get all fidgety when I say I'm gonna call you Sarus ... and yeah, yeah, yeah, I know what you're gonna say, and maybe you're right, but just shut your goddamn snout and come when I call." He is silent for a minute or more and then rolls to his side and reaches down for the dog's block head.

The dog sits up to meet his hand. "Sarus," Charlie whispers. "That's your name now. I looked it up. For the record, it's a beautiful Asian crane, and also the name of some Goth chieftain. Take your pick. But it's Sarus. And don't fuckin' think I'm calling you Sarah."

***

Unlike he would have done previously, Charlie patiently and stoically withstands with some grace all the kind gestures, all the well-intentioned good wishes. But a week later when Andrew shows up in the late afternoon and says, "I can't believe she's gone," Charlie reaches for Sarus's block head, looks up, and, without warning, speaks in his old voice. "She's not dead, Andrew, she just slipped through the veil. She's here." He points at the double doorway into the studio as if she were standing there, just checking her watch.

Andrew looks at the empty doorway. "No one is there."

Charlie isn't going to argue. He presses his lips together and lets his eyes fall on the dog, just then scratching behind his ear.

"No one is there, Dad," Andrew insists. "Mom is dead. I found her on the kitchen floor ten days ago. She's dead."

When Charlie looks up through the still air, Andrew is staring at him, full of the kind of pity that makes his skin crawl.

"There she goes," Charlie says.

"Who goes?"

Charlie drops his chin to his chest and, without looking, closes a folder with a series of prints from 1989. "Me." And a few moments later he adds, "I'm sorry, Andrew. I gotta get out of here, son." He places his palms on the drafting table and pushes himself up with a grunt. "I am sorry."

"But where you going?" Andrew sounds like the eight-year-old he once was, so much like his own eight-year-old he left back home, whining about being left behind.

"I ... I am sorry. Let's just say I just need a little time to myself. I'm going to have to walk through this veil all alone.

You and your brother are going to have to let me do this in my own time, in my own way. So, move aside, Andrew. I'm gonna get in the Jeep and drive for a while."

Andrew does not move. "When will you be back?"

Charlie shrugs. He has no idea. But he does know that stepping through this membrane takes no courage. Just one plodding step. Then the next. "A couple of hours. Don't worry about me."

At the doorway, he places both hands on Andrew's shoulders, moves him gently to the side, and walks around him, leaving him standing haplessly in the hallway. And without another word, Charlie strides through the kitchen and out the side door. Seconds later he is backing the Jeep out of the garage and heading up Ledge Road, Sarus curled up in the passenger seat at his side.

The only thing Charlie Messina can think about in that moment is biting into a lobster roll.

First, though, he feels his breast pocket and looks down at the gas gauge.

***

Charlie can see—or at least imagine—the blood draining out of Manny Cardozo's narrow, pimply face the moment the boy recognizes the Jeep pulling up to the pumps.

"Y'know," Charlie says to Sarus, "I should just play it safe and use my credit card at the pump. Let the kid off the hook." Sarus sits up and looks out the windowless half door. "But with everything that's happened, I think that's a dishonest way to set things right. Don't you think?"

Sarus leaps out of his side of the Jeep as Charlie opens his half door and swivels his feet to the concrete. "Hey! Where you going?"

The dog doesn't even turn his head, just lopes over to the sidewalk, pees on a parking meter, walks up to the STOP sign, and sits.

Charlie is tempted to lumber after him, but he knows that he'd look like a doddering fool chasing an invisible dog, and, besides, he knows the damn hound can just slip behind the veil and disappear whenever he decides to. Better to just take care of the problem at hand. Yanking open the glass door to the too-cool convenience store, he walks up to the counter with a palm in the air and what he figures is a disarming grin on his face. "Bet you thought you'd never see me again."

If Manny's face hadn't actually drained of all color when Charlie pulled up to the pumps, it now grows wide-eyed and ghostly as he glances over Charlie's shoulder to the bays.

Charlie turns to see Raul Cardozo standing in the doorway, clearly caught in the neurological vacuum between recognizing someone he should know and realizing who the intruder might be.

"Hello, Mr. Cardozo," Charlie begins in the hopes of intercepting the memory and the moment of full recognition. "Just stopping in for some gas and a pack of cancer sticks." He grins and points toward the Jeep.

The diversion doesn't work. Cardozo points a thick, blackened index finger. "I thought I told you to stay the fuck out of here."

"You did, but I thought ... well, I thought we were both mature enough to look past a ... what? ... a most unfortunate misunderstanding."

"Get the fuck out of here."

"I will. I promise." He holds up his right palm. "I just want to get some gas and a pack of Luckies—and I'll be out of here in a jiff."

Cardozo takes a step forward. Then another. He points to the door. "I said get the fuck out of my gas station."

Charlie peers out the glass door and up the sidewalk to the STOP sign at the corner. Sarus is gone. And before he can stop himself, he's feeling like he needs some kind of triumph after all his pain and misery, so he points a thick finger back at Cardozo and demands some respect. "Listen, jackass, I just came here for some gas and a pack of cigarettes—and that's what I goddamn plan on getting."

Now Cardozo is up in his grill and spitting. "I said get the fuck outa here!"

Which is when Charlie, defying all the howling voices in his head, defying the realities of age, pushes the shorter man hard on his shoulders and watches as Raul Cardozo stumbles back into the rack of chips, knocking it over, tripping over his own feet trying to avoid crushing the merchandise.

Cardozo sits momentarily dazed on the filthy linoleum.

Satisfied that he has made his point, Charlie turns around and is about to tell Manny that he wants twenty dollars' worth of regular and a pack of Luckies when he is tackled from behind, rammed belly first into the counter. Lighters and little power drinks go flying as Charlie collapses to the floor, the younger, stronger man grabbing him by the shirt and rolling him over, making a fist and punching the old man once, twice, blood spurting from Charlie's nose, something—a tooth?—caught between gum and tongue.

Cardozo stands then, face bloodless, chest heaving, and drags the heavier old man by the collar to the door. "I said get the fuck outa here." He glares at Manny then and turns to go back into the bays. "You. Get this piece of shit out of here right now."

Manny waits until the metal door closes behind his dad, then helps Charlie up. Brings him some bunched-up paper towels for his bloody nose.

Charlie spits the tooth into his palm, looks at it, and drops it into his breast pocket. "That is not it at all, that is not what I meant, at all," he says into the wadded up and bloodied paper towel.

Taking him by the elbow, Manny nods over at the closed door and says, "I really think you should go, mister."

Charlie shrugs him off his arm. "I'm going. I'm going. But you tell your old man we're not done with this."

The boy scurries back behind the counter, grabs a pack of Luckies off the shelf, and hands it to him. "Please, mister, take this and go. We don't need any trouble here."

Charlie smacks away the pack. Rubs his sore chin. "Well, tell your—" He stops when he sees panic roil the boy's face. "Okay. Manny … just tell him we're not done here." He pushes open the glass door.

"What are you going to …," the boy starts, dark eyes glistening. Pleading. His mouth twisted.

"I don't know what I'm going to do," Charlie says, the glass door closing slowly behind him as he lumbers over to the Jeep.

Sarus is not in the passenger's seat. Before he puts the key into the ignition, Charlie scans the station, the sidewalk, the cross streets. "So, you're gonna fuckin' desert me, too."

And when there is no answer, he feels for his cigarettes, but there is nothing in his pocket except a small pebble that he figures is his tooth. He drives to the BP on Route 138, tosses the bloody paper towel into the garbage can at the gas tanks, and, offering up a swollen-lipped, gapped-tooth smile to the utterly disinterested young woman behind the counter, buys a new pack of Luckies.

From there, a right onto 238 and a left onto Broadway, and Charlie parks in front of the Newport Police Station, engine rumbling, still pondering whether he is going to report the attack or just do the "mature" thing and chalk the whole thing up to his own temporary insanity caused by his grief over Sarah's death. Any way he parses it, though, Charlie can hear Sarah calling him a jackass from beyond the veil.

After sitting there for a while, Charlie rips the cellophane off the Luckies, tears the metallic paper back, and, pounding the pack against his open palm, pinches a single cigarette out between his lips, where blood has already dried at the corners. He lights the cigarette with some matches he finds on the dashboard, inhales, and waits, still trying to decide if he should go inside and lodge a complaint.

He recalls the panicked look on Manny's pimply face and takes another drag, looks over at the steps leading up to the station when he sees Sarus meandering down the sidewalk, lifting his leg at a parking meter, sniffing the grass, eventually sitting down on the curb next to the Jeep.

From his perch behind the steering wheel Charlie can't see the dog, but he knows he is there. He wants to say, *I was so worried I would never see you again*, but what he says is, "What the hell was that all about back there? You afraid of a little confrontation? You a chicken dog ... puck, puck, puck, puck, puck? And what the hell are you doing here now?"

Sarus jumps over the half door and is back on the seat a moment later. Snout on his paws.

"What is this? Some passive-aggressive attempt to get me to stay in the car and just let Cardozo get away with assaulting me?"

The dog yawns.

"I know what Sarah would say," he says, taking a long drag, then flicking the still burning cigarette out into the street. "She'd say, 'Let well enough alone, Charlie.' But that woman never understood these things. She never understood setting things right. Always saying—" And there was her voice in his head again: *Don't be a jackass, Charlie.*

A moment or a lifetime later he feels the shadow before noticing the police officer standing next to the Jeep, a cigarette butt between his thumb and forefinger. "I could give you a citation for littering, you know."

Charlie glances at the passenger seat—where the dog is wagging his tail—and then up at the policeman. Tempted to say, *Give me the fuckin' citation*, he shrugs instead, offers his sheepish smile, and extends his palm. The officer, who can't be more than thirty, scowls and drops the butt in his hand. Charlie quickly transfers it into the tiny metal ashtray.

"What happened to your nose?" the cop asks.

Charlie shakes his head. "Tripped over my own feet getting out of bed this morning."

"You okay?"

Pressing his lips together to dam up the rising sob, Charlie nods.

"Well, don't let me see you do that again," the officer says, and without another word, turns and walks off across the street.

"Up yours," Charlie mumbles under his breath as soon as the beefed-up, flak-jacketed cop has waddled across the yellow line. And when the cop is safely on the other side of the street, he jams the shifter into first, rides the clutch, and lurches into traffic, too quickly shifting into second, third, fourth and is finally headed uptown with the traffic, over to Route 24, past New Bedford, and straight into Wareham, Massachusetts, where he finally stops carping about Raul Cardozo and that smug piece-of-shit cop.

***

Passing the WELCOME TO SANDWICH, MA (INCORPORATED 1639) sign, and thinking, *all those dead souls since 1639*, he drives straight to Gertie's Roadside Rest. Jams on the brakes as soon as he hits the parking lot gravel for no other reason than he likes the sound. Then turns off the engine, waits while it diesels for a while, and looks all around at the empty parking lot.

Sarus leaps out of the Jeep and disappears beneath the door. "Hey," Charlie growls and then quickly realizes the futility of controlling that animal, the patent absurdity of applying the laws of one dimension to another.

He sits there waiting for the boy, Joey, to come pedaling into the parking lot. Somehow he knows the kid will show up.

But first a lobster roll.

Charlie glances in the small rearview mirror, grimaces, pulls out a hanky, spits on it, and wipes off the dried blood around his nose and mouth. Looks in the mirror again. Spits once more and, checking the mirror, wipes and wipes and wipes it all away. Checks one more time and leans over with a grunt to shove the handkerchief into his back pocket.

In the momentary silence that follows a truck passing on the highway, Joey is still not there, so Charlie eases himself out of the Jeep and walks over to the window with the sign ORDER HERE. Which is when he reads the computer-generated sign on the window itself:

CLOSED FOR THE SEASON. SEE YOU IN APRIL

It takes Charlie a few seconds to place himself in time. So much had gone on since he and Mason left for Dylan's fall tour at the end of September, Columbus, Toledo, Ann Arbor, Bloomington, Iowa City, Madison … and Sarah. *Oh.* He places his hands flat on the empty counter, lowers his head, and feels his swollen upper lip begin to tremble.

"Whatsamatter?" comes that girlish voice from behind him.

Charlie wipes the tears away from his eyes with his knuckles, pulls out the bloody handkerchief from his back pocket, blows his nose, and finally turns around to find the kid, Joey, straddling his bike.

"You crying?"

Charlie smiles at the boy before speaking. "I was sad that I couldn't get a lobster roll."

The kid nods. "There's a new McDonald's up the road." He points down Route 6. "Better 'n this."

94

"It's not the same, kid. I had my heart set on a lobster roll."

Still straddling the bike, Joey shifts from one foot to another, makes a funny scrunched up face, and says, "Ain't nothin' to cry about, but maybe I could get my ma to make you a roll. Y'know, she's got tons of that stuff in the freezer for the winter." He blows out his cheeks in disgust and points the other way.

Charlie laughs. Maybe for the first time in days. "I was only teasing you, kid." He looks away, his eyes filling again, his voice just above a whisper. "My wife died a week ago. That's why I'm sad."

Joey nods. Scrunches his lips to the side. "Sorry."

"You remember me?"

The kid nods again. "Yes, sir."

"You just saying that?"

"No. You're the one who bought me the hot-fudge sundae at Ben and Jerry's ... two times." A smirk followed by the shadow of a scowl moves across his face. "And you're the one who takes the Lord's name in vain."

"Right. Right." Charlie nods and then nods some more, waiting for words to form in his brain to keep the conversation going. He doesn't know why, but he doesn't want the kid to go away. "So why aren't you in school?"

"I dunno. Superintemments Day or something." He turns the handlebars, stands, and places his sneaker on the pedal as if he were about to ride away.

"So ... what are you going to do on your day off?"

There is the scowl again. "Nothing."

"But why are you here?"

"Well, I was on my way to my friend Bruce Hill's house"— he points up Route 6— "and I seen your Jeep."

Charlie laughs. "And you thought there might be another ice cream in your future?"

The kid shrugs. "I just seen your Jeep, that's all."

"Can't kid a kidder, kid. I know what you're up to."

Joey shrugs again and looks to the side. "When'd you get a new dog, mister?"

PART III

"I get the impression sometimes that a play arrives in a sequence of events that I have no control over."

—Tom Stoppard

Chapter Ten (or One)

"You see the dog? You really see the dog?"

Joey looked at him as if he was crazy. "Course I seen it. I ain't blind! He's sittin' right over there in the passenger seat. Anyway, what's wrong with your nose?"

Charlie cupped his swollen nose and said, "Well, ain't this a goddamn hoot."

"You're still not s'posed to take the Lord's name in vain, mister. I told you, it just ain't right."

"Right. And I'm sorry. I am sorry, kid. But let me just check with you again … you see the dog?"

Joey rolled his eyes. "What else would I be seein'? And why's your nose all swolled and bloody?"

Charlie ignored him. "Describe it."

"It's swolled and bloody."

"No, no, no, no, no … the dog: describe it."

"It's a dog."

"How big is it?"

Joey's eyes narrowed. "About this high," he said, his right hand just above the old man's knee.

"And what color is he?"

"Are you blind, mister?"

"No. I'm seein' just fine. But I'm just curious to know what you see when you look at the dog."

Joey opened his eyes in an exaggerated fashion, turned the bike handlebars, and, sounding like he was talking to a stupid younger brother, said, "He's black. And he's fat." And then he grinned. "Just like you."

Charlie laughed. "I'm gonna give you a pass on that. But ...?"

"I passed! I'm in fourth grade!"

"No ... I meant what else do you see?"

"I dunno. What happened to your nose?"

Inhaling through his battered nostrils, Charlie turned away and said, "I walked into a sliding glass door that I thought was open."

Joey laughed, making donkey honks.

"It wasn't so funny at the time," Charlie said, rolling his hand around several times. "Go on."

"Go on, what?"

"The dog?"

"Oh. Well, he's got flippy-floppy ears." Sarus sat up, his thick black tail wagging, and jumped out of the Jeep.

"C'mere, boy," Joey motioned, and Sarus came wiggling over to the boy's thigh. Joey swished his hand around the dog's head.

"You can feel him?"

Joey rolled his eyes. "You musta scrambled your brains when you hit that door."

"But you can feel him?"

"Course I can feel him. Does he fetch or anything?"

"Nah. Not that I know of."

"You ain't tried?"

Charlie scrunched up his lips and shook his head. "I'm not much of a dog trainer. Anyway, I just got him."

"You just got him? He's old! What'd you do ... get him out of the pound?"

"No. He just showed up one day."

"From where?"

"Don't know. Showed up at my back door one morning." He looked hard at the boy and then decided to just come out with it. "I think he's always been around, I just never noticed him before."

Joey scowled but quickly nodded as if he understood, and then loped over to the side of the shuttered lobster-roll stand. "Wait!" he called back over his shoulder, reaching under the counter, and he pulled out a dirty tennis ball and held it up.

"What the hell is that doing there?"

The kid glared at him.

"Sorry, kid. I need to watch my mouth. So why is there a tennis ball under the counter?"

Joey looked down at his sneakers and mumbled. "Belonged to my old dog Chester. He liked to chase balls." A few moments later he added, "Almost forgot I stashed it there."

"I'm sorry, kid."

"About what?"

"About your dog dying."

The boy nodded. "Happens. What's his name?"

Charlie inhaled and exhaled through his nose before answering. "Sarus," he said.

The boy glared again. "That's a dumb name."

"Can't do anything about it. That's his name."

"Can't be his name."

"Why not?"

The boy shook his head. "I dunno. He don't look like no Sarus."

"Doesn't, and ... well, it is. He is. Sarus."

Joey narrowed his eyes and held up the tennis ball in the cup of his hand. Cocked his arm. "No matter. But I know it ain't the right name. Anyways, does he fetch?"

"Give it a ride," Charlie said, full of the kind of wonder he hadn't known since he was Joey's age, pointing toward the grassy patch behind the stand. The boy tossed the ball, and both of them watched it bounce once, twice, then roll toward the back of the lot. Sarus didn't move.

"I guess he don't fetch," the boy said.

"Guess not." Then Charlie remembered the Milk Bones in the glove box, the ones he had kept for BadBreath. "You ... go in the Jeep and open the glove box." He was waving a thick index finger up and down. "Bring me back a couple of dog biscuits."

Joey did as he was told. Handed over the bones and waited. "Now go get me the ball."

Joey ran out to the grassy patch, tossed the ball back, and a few moments later, at Charlie's urging, held up the ball with one hand, and with the other, he held a biscuit between thumb and forefinger. "You want this?" Joey said to the dog.

Sarus wagged his tail. Joey tossed the ball toward the same grassy spot in the yard.

The dog didn't move. Just sat there wagging his tail.

"No fetchee, no biscuit."

The dog didn't move. Joey handed the biscuits back to Charlie. "I guess he don't fetch."

The dog then stood, stretched, and trotted out behind the building, past the ball, past the broken fence line, and then disappeared in the woods.

"Where's he going?" Charlie asked, as if the boy should know something he didn't.

"Don't know." The boy looked around. "But I gotta get going, too. Bruce Hill's mom said—" He didn't finish. And with that he picked his bike up off the gravel lot and, leaning into the handlebars, raced a few yards, hopped on the banana seat, and pedaled off.

Seconds later Charlie was standing all alone at the deserted lobster-roll stand, looking up and down Route 6, wondering if he had made up the whole damn thing. Wondering if this meant he'd never see Sarus again. And wondering if he was going crazy.

***

After a while with no answers coming from anywhere—and no dog in the vicinity—Charlie was back in the Jeep, backing out of the empty lot, as always comforted by the engine's whine, and then heading back home, eyebrows clenched, but every once in a while, a smile breaking the surface of his pained face.

Stopped at the light on Swift's Beach Road, he realized that he was no longer afraid that Sarus was missing—or that he'd never see him again. Or even that he was batshit crazy. In that seemingly inconsequential moment, he knew he would run into Sarus again before too long. It really was just about walking through one veil or another. And maybe it was just walking through one veil *and* then walking through another. The only question was how to get there—or there—on your own. And now more important ... much, much, much, more important ... was how to get to Sarah.

A moment later Sarus was back sitting in the passenger seat, shiny snout out the window, floppy ears flipping around in the breeze. "Hey, how'd you do that?" And a breath or two later, "No, no, no, no, no ... it's not 'How'd you do that?' ... it's 'How the hell did I do that? ... HOW THE FUCK DID I DO THAT!?" he called out to the heavens.

Minutes and miles sliding under the Jeep like it was in some kind of wind tunnel, passing through Mattapoisett without any memory of East Marion or Marion. "And how the hell did that happen?"

The dog didn't move, nose out the window. Panting when the light turned red. "And as long as I'm wondering ... maybe you can tell me how the hell can I get through to her slice of time and space? I'm talking about Sarah in case you didn't know."

Sarus barked at something on the other side of the intersection, but it was impossible to make out what had gotten him riled. "And another thing ... how did that kid see you? What the hell was that all about?"

The light changed; Charlie popped the clutch and the dog lost traction, slipping and sliding against the seat before getting himself composed again, then sitting up, looking straight out the windshield.

"Sorry. I just have so many questions, and I never know whether you're around—or I think you're around. I'm not even sure that when I rub your head, I'm really rubbing your head! And now you've got me so fuckin' confused I'm not sure whether I'm dead or alive—or even if anyone ever really dies."

A couple hundred yards down the road, he braked, reaching over to steady the dog like he used to do with the kids, and pulled off onto the shoulder. Looked over at the dog. "Am I dead?"

The dog curled up on the torn seat, snout between his front paws.

"And well ... so what if I am?"

***

By the time he had made his way back to Newport, Charlie was feeling a whole lot better about life—and death—and was even tempted to stop by the Sunoco to see if he could try to patch things up with Manny and his old man, Raul. But then he reached up and felt his swollen nose—and remembered the taste of blood—and drove on to the empty house on Ledge Road.

Now pleased with his own restraint, he walked through the kitchen door and stood two steps in, just looking around and listening. For a few seconds he was sure that Andrew was still there. Maybe even hoping Andrew was there. But no one was home.

He was alone.

He dropped the keys on the kitchen counter, producing a sound he'd heard thousands of times over the years that he and Sarah had lived on Ledge Road and without ever once taking notice of how comforting and beautiful it was.

And now, out of that nowhere, what an ache it created. He reached over to pick up the keys again, just to drop them one more time. But he let his hand hover there for a moment, unable or unwilling to break the plane, and shoved his hand into his pocket.

From there he wandered into the living room. Stood in the arched doorway and looked around. The floral couch. The peach wing chairs. The stone fireplace. Sarah's carved birds on the mantle. His 1997 black-and-white photograph of the marsh over the mantle.

Briefly considering going into the room and dropping into the couch, he was seized with fear that once he sat down, he might never have the strength to get up again. There was no place to go but back to the studio.

He stood in a doorway. Locked eyes on the piles of prints lined up in chronological order on the metal cabinets next to the worktable. The old jeweler's monocle. A contact sheet of the kid Joey from the lobster-roll joint last summer; another one from the first encounter at the Sunoco. Raul Cardozo with a tire iron in his hand. The Nauset Knoll shot, Sarah at the round table on the sloping lawn.

Impossible to cross the threshold and walk in.

Elbowing in front of the events of the last few hours was a memory of the partygoers in Buñuel's *The Discreet Charm of the Bourgeoisie*. And not especially how they were stuck in the parlor, unable to break the invisible plane, just the futility of the whole thing.

Then it was back to the kitchen. Sitting down at the table— a woven placemat and folded linen napkin in front of him, a vase with one peony in the center, probably set there by Cecilia. The refrigerator motor kicked on. A distant sound of newspaper pages being turned.

And when he looked up across the table, Sarah was sitting there, reading the *New York Times*.

Thinking to check the date on the paper, he instantly forgot as he uttered her name. "Sarah ..."

She didn't look up.

Even though he already knew she was not going to talk, he spoke to her as if midway into a conversation: "I mean, what the hell am I going to do without you?"

She turned the page, flattened the paper with her left hand, picked up a cup of coffee that hadn't been there seconds ago in her right hand, took a sip, put it down, and went on reading.

"Yeah, yeah, yeah, I get it—I get it, you're not going to acknowledge my presence. It's not allowed. Right? I get it. The big turd on the other side of the veil has rules? Right?"

Sarah glared at something, but she was just looking through him.

"Well, just give me a sign that you know I'm here." She turned the page with her left hand and flattened the paper with her right. And reaching blindly for the cup, she went on reading.

"A sign, Sarah. That's all I'm asking."

She looked at her watch and then over to the kitchen door and out to the breezeway.

"Well, pretend I'm not here, if that's what you must do. But let me tell you about the kid seeing the dog. I mean, this is big, Sarah—B-I-G!"

The kitchen was flooded with light, the bloody orange light of a spectacular sunset over the Sound, and Charlie leapt up out of the chair, finger pointing at the vision across the table. "Well, fuckin' A, I got it! You don't know I'm here! I'm in your world but you're not in mine!" Reaching down then to find the dog's block head and flopping the ears back and forth, Charlie didn't care whether the dog was there or not. The dog was there.

So Sarah was there!

Everything grew still then, like in a photograph, his hand just over the dog's skull, breath stilled, heart in between beats, and Charlie found himself pushing back the chair and standing, his thighs banging against the table, the table legs scraping along the wood floor.

He was walking around the table. Standing behind Sarah. Hands shaking. Reaching for her shoulders, already smelling the sweetness of her hair. She instantly disappeared as he knew she would, stumbling forward, catching himself on the back of the wooden chair, a laugh swelling up out of his entrails. "Oh my God, this is good."

The kitchen door swung open and banged into the counter. "What's good, Dad?" Andrew. He sounded alarmed. Of course. "And why are you leaning on ... *that* chair? Are you all right?"

For a second or two it was not clear if Andrew was really there or not. Or where he had come from. "It's you," Charlie said.

"Of course, it's me. But what's good? Are you all right? I heard you barking all the way from the driveway—"

"Barking?"

"Just a turn of phrase. You were talking. Loud."

"I'm fine, Andrew. I don't know what I was yelling about."

"Oh my God," Andrew said, pointing at Charlie's bloody, puffy face, "what the hell happened to you?"

Charlie reached up and felt his swollen and tender nose. "Walked right into a sliding glass door. How's that for a jackass move?"

Andrew didn't laugh like Joey had. He shoved his hands in his coat pockets and walked over to the table to pull out

Charlie's chair. "Sit down, Dad. You look like Gene Fullmer."
A smirk flickered across his face.

"I'm fine. I'm fine. But Gene Fullmer? Gene Fullmer? What'd you do, just pull that name right out of your ass?"

Andrew shrugged. "I don't know. Just came to me. When I was a kid you used to talk about him and Carmen Bas-something—"

"Basilio," Charlie said. "So?"

"You used to show me and Dylan photographs of both of them—faces pounded like veal. Like you look right now." He pointed down toward the chair. "Sit. Let me see your face."

"I'm fine, son. But I gotta do some work before I lose the daylight." He turned away and nodded toward the studio. "I'm fine, Andrew. You really don't have to worry about me. I'm fine."

"But I am worried about you. I just came by to say, why don't you come stay at my house for a couple of days? I know that Cecilia would love to dote on you. I don't know why, but she actually seems to adore you." He lowered his voice then as if what was to come next was a stage aside. "Never been able to figure that one out."

Charlie could feel a shadow passing across his battered mug. "Thank you, Andrew, but that's probably the last thing I need right now. I love your wife, too, but I'd probably sink so far into her kind care that I might never get up again. You know what I mean?"

Andrew took a deep breath before he nodded.

"You go home, son. I really do appreciate your concern, but I got some things I got to walk through." Charlie laughed. "I meant things I gotta work through. And I gotta work through them all by myself. Give Cecilia—and the kids—a hug for me."

Andrew didn't move.

"You should go home now."

Andrew's eyes grew watery.

"Go!" Charlie fake-growled, swinging his arm around like he was pitching a softball. Then again, "Go," but a little softer this time.

Andrew's chest rose and fell. Rose and fell. "Okay," he said finally, "but I'm going to call you tomorrow morning, and ... and you'll come over for dinner tomorrow night."

Charlie nodded, full of love for his boy. "Hey," he called over, "I'm sorry I've been such a pain in the ass since—" He didn't finish, looking away, out the window to the marsh. Then just above a whisper, "Since Joni died."

Now Andrew nodded, a tear sliding down his cheek. "I'll see you tomorrow."

And when Andrew left, Charlie went to the bedroom, packed an overnight bag, and headed for the Jeep.

Chapter Eleven (or Two)

"Dad?"

"Dylan—"

"Where the hell are you?" Dylan yelled.

Charlie held the phone away from his ear.

"You got everyone crazy with worry around here. I had to cancel—"

"Sorry," Charlie interrupted. "Sorry."

Then there was silence. Charlie smiled a smile Dylan couldn't see. "It's an old story ... a search for love and glory ..."

"Not funny."

"How about, I went out for a cup of coffee and I guess I just kept driving. Next thing I knew I was down on Sanibel."

"Florida?" Dylan gasped. "Fucking Florida? What the hell? I thought you hated everything about Florida."

"Your mother loved it."

After a deep breathy sniff of air, Dylan said, "Mom's dead, Pop."

Charlie looked to the side. Inhaled. Exhaled. Reached for the pack of Luckies. "I know."

"I've been ... we've been calling you ... every goddamn day, several times a day. Your friend Mason and I have been driving around Newport all morning looking for clues."

In the background, Charlie could hear Mason's distant though distinct voice: "Put it on speaker." Then a moment later, a full throated "You are a bigger asshole than I ever thought possible."

"I turned off the phone. I needed…" Then there was another silence. Three men, 1,500 miles apart, chests heaving, not knowing what to say.

"Are you all right?"

Charlie struck a match, took the puckering suck of that first toke, and broke through that veil. "I am. And I really am sorry, Dylan. I'm sorry I caused all of you so much worry. I wasn't thinking; I just had to get away."

Mason broke in. "You're a goddamn schmuck!"

"Yeah, yeah, yeah." Then more silence.

More quivering breaths, until Dylan said more gently, "So where are you? Why there? Did you call Andrew?"

"No, not yet. I don't know why, but I figured you might be a little more understanding."

"I don't know what to say."

Then Mason, "I know what to say. You're a miserable human being, Charlie Messina!"

"I guess I was wrong."

"You were dead wrong. So where in the hell are you?"

"I told you, Sanibel."

"Sanibel?" Dylan shouted as if it had just sunk in.

His voice felt like a horn going off in Charlie's ear. It took a few more breaths to be able to speak. "A little cottage court on the north end of the island, The Periwinkle Dolphin or some such stupid Florida name."

"Are you coming home?"

Another pause.

"I am. I am. I got this place for another two weeks and…" Again, he couldn't finish, glancing over at the empty passenger seat, Sarus curled up on the tiny bench seat behind it. "I'll be home in two weeks, give or take."

Then silence. But Charlie could hear everything going on in Dylan's van. Could see it all happening like it was a film. Opening the glove box, grabbing a pack of Marlboros.

Flipping open the top. Pulling out a cigarette and a Bic lighter. Slipping the filter between his lips, spinning the dial on the lighter.

Charlie waited for the exhale, knowing the smoke was rising out the window of Dylan's prized '86 Vanagon.

"What the hell were you thinking?"

"I don't know that I was doing much thinking, just driving through a bunch of increasingly southern states, then stopping here ... getting through each day. And for the time being, Dylan, that's pretty much the best I can do."

"Are you really all right?"

"I am. I just miss your mother more than you can imagine. More than I ever imagined."

"Okay. Now do me a favor and call my brother. He's been out of his goddamn mind since you disappeared. He's ... well, what? A lot nicer than we are? Likes the feel of a hair shirt? Whatever. He thinks it's all his fault."

"His fault? He's a jackass, your brother."

Dylan choked out a laugh. "Well, there's one thing we can agree on." Then they were silent again. "Call me as soon as you get your sorry ass back to Newport."

"I will."

"And fucking answer the phone if I call."

"Roger."

Then Mason again, "You're an asshole."

"Roger. Bye ..."

But that didn't end the call. Dylan had turned off the speaker, and now it was just the two of them breathing into cell phones.

Charlie took the phone from his cheek and looked at the screen. Pressed the red button. Hit the text icon in the upper right, his thick index finger pressing A ... then N ... and once Andrew's name and number appeared, Charlie punched in the following message in caps:

I'M FINE. ITS NOT YOUR DAMN FAULT. ILL SEE YOU SOON. He added an X—then an O—then deleted it—then wrote I LOVE YOU, DAD. Then pressed Send.

***

Two weeks later, with the old Jeep thrumming and humming along in the right lane of I-75 approaching Sarasota and Sarus asleep, Charlie was singing over and over—and way off key—the refrain from Simon and Garfunkel's "America."

And all the while he was thinking about Joey and Manny and what the hell was so interesting about a couple of mostly uninteresting boys right out of central casting.

He was interrupted by the cell phone quacking sort of like a duck, Sarah's tones. Picked it up and Mason's mug was on the screen. He looked around at the world speeding by to his right and left, then in the rearview mirror, and finally he pressed the green button. No hello, no accusations, just "Where are you?"

"I dunno ... coming up on Sarasota in an hour or so, I think."

"Good. Glad I got you before ... well, anyway, keep going up to Tampa International. You can pick me up at three-thirty."

"What?" Charlie shouted over the road noise.

"I'm arriving on Delta Flight Two-Eight-Seven out of Boston—three-thirty. I'll meet you at the curb."

"Where you going?"

"What'd I just say? I'm going to Tampa, you doddering old fool. I'm long past beginning to worry about you. You've crossed over into the realm of the chronic pains in my ass. You're right up there in the narcissist ward with my ex-wives."

"Y'know, I have never understood why I'm friends with you. Even back in Williamstown when we were supposed to be buddies. What the hell are you doing in Tampa?"

"Getting a ride with you back to Newport."

Charlie yanked the steering wheel right and pulled onto the shoulder of the highway. The Jeep skidded to a gravelly stop. It took a few seconds for Charlie to compose himself. "Why the bloody hell are you doing that?"

"It's the only way I can be sure that you're coming home. And it might be the only way I can keep your sons from committing patricide."

"I don't know what to say."

"Don't say anything. Just remember: three-thirty, Tampa International, Delta Flight Two-Eight-Seven."

"No way in hell I'm going to pick you up."

"Three-thirty, Tampa International," Mason repeated. "Delta Flight Two-Eight-Seven out of Beantown."

"I'm not picking you up, Mason."

"Three-thirty, Tampa International, Delta Flight Two-Eight-Seven."

"Not a snowball's chance in hell."

The line went dead. Mason's picture had disappeared when Charlie glared at the screen. He turned to Sarus, who was just then licking his balls, shrugged, and said, "I guess Mason's gonna join us."

***

Forty minutes later, just as Charlie pulled past the gate into the short-term parking garage at Tampa International, the Jeep felt empty. And when he looked to his right, Sarus had disappeared and was no longer curled up on the back seat.

"I don't get this," he muttered, all the while steering the whining Jeep in second gear up around the curving ramp. "If I can see the goddamn dog, why can't I see her?" Not that he expected anyone—or anything—to be talking to him. "Sarah," he added pointlessly.

Then he parked right under the D6 sign, killed the engine, pulled a folded 4X6 index card and pen from his breast pocket, wrote down D6, and returned the card and pen to his pocket. "I get it," he began again in a whisper, quickly raising his voice to a conversational tone, "but I don't fucking get who makes the connections. Is the dog walking through the veil, or am I? "

There was no answer, of course, but Charlie stopped himself from carrying on the conversation when a corporate-looking middle-aged couple walked up to the Lexus parked in front of him. He heard the beep of the fob unlocking the doors and then watched as the man tossed a puce-colored suitcase in the back seat, closed the door, opened the driver side door, slid in, powered down the windows, and said something to the woman.

She howled with laughter, loud enough for the parking garage echo to reach him, slapping her hands repeatedly on the dashboard. Charlie knew—or thought he knew—exactly what that yuppie-shit had said to that woman; in fact, he was already mouthing it to himself: "If you ever find me sitting in car in a public parking lot talking to myself, shoot me."

A moment later Charlie was pivoting out of the Jeep, about to give the couple a piece of his mind, when he looked over and saw that they had already backed up and were headed toward the exit.

That's when the phone dinged—DELTA BAGGAGE CLAIM shouted on the screen. "Oh Christ," Charlie grumbled, walking over to the elevators with Sarus and striding across the ramp and into the terminal, where he spotted Mason standing in front of the automatic door typing something into his phone.

"Too late, jackass," Charlie called out.

Mason looked up. "Well, well, well, Charles Messina, aren't you a sight ... for sore, myopic eyes, that is. Those stained cut-off khakis, that ratty BadBreath t-shirt, and those worn-to-shit Birkenstocks place you somewhere in the cultural Stone Age."

Charlie stopped a few feet away and looked his old friend up and down. Long silver hair pulled back into a ponytail, white linen shirt, white cotton drawstring pants, flip-flops. "And you look like some kind of New Age nursing home gigolo."

Mason smiled. "Good to see you, my friend."

"You too, I guess."

"Oh, come on, you old fucktard, I'm happy to see you." He leaned down and picked up a small leather bag with one hand, reaching over to pat Charlie on the shoulder with the other, and then pointed out beyond the circular door to the curb. "Let's go get a drink down by the water somewhere, and I'll tell you what's what—and you can tell me what the hell you've been thinking for the last few weeks."

Chapter Twelve (or Three): An Hour Later

"You think this heap is gonna make it back home?" Mason called over the road noise and the cracked muffler.

Charlie glanced behind him to see if Sarus was there—he wasn't—and yelled, "This heap will still be around to tow your girly piece of Italian frufru to the scrapyard."

Which was the full extent of their conversation until they passed a sign for Ocala, Charlie overcome by despair about going home ... to what? nothing really, a worn-out life in the frozen salt marsh, just one day after the next, one day stumbling deeper and deeper into the slowly melting ice among the reeds until the water was up to his neck, horseflies around his ears, ripples from the sound lapping at his upturned mouth. He signaled, braked, and veered off the highway onto the gravel shoulder.

Mason glanced over, eyes wide. "Engine problems?"

"No." Both hands on the wheel, Charlie didn't know where to start, though Mason was likely the one person in the entire world who would understand, who might even be able to explain it all to him, the one who was now waiting patiently for some explanation that Charlie couldn't find inside of himself, except to say, "I don't want to go home, Mason."

Mason nodded.

"Or maybe it's that I just don't want to go home right now. I don't want to be cold,"—he paused and added a few beats later—"in that house, all alone."

Mason turned away and looked straight ahead through the windshield. "Well, shit then, my brother, let's stay down here for a while. You know me, I've got nothing going on ... and no prospects ... nothing but a weekly boring-ass lunch date with some old cantankerous fart I used to know." He smiled but kept staring through the windshield.

"I know him, too."

"And I'm pretty sure I've worn out my welcome with the two women left in the solar system who don't think I'm a cad."

"They all think you're a cad, Mason. Don't fool yourself." Charlie reached over and squeezed his friend's knee.

They might have sat there in the rumbling Jeep on the gravel shoulder of I-75 for hours more, but Charlie heard a bark and swung around to the back seat. Sarus wasn't there. "You hear that?"

"Hear what?"

"A dog barking ... like somewhere close by." He craned his neck to look behind the Jeep.

"I can't hear anything but the engine in this macho man jalopy. But I've been just sitting here thinking that we can drive back to Sanibel and pool our money and stick around for the holidays."

"You didn't hear a dog?"

"No! Are you listening? I said maybe we can stick around through the holidays, maybe a little longer." He switched his weight and reached into his pocket for his phone, punched in some digits, and, smiling, turned back to Charlie, but he wasn't behind the wheel. He was behind the rattling Jeep, thick hand over his eyebrows, looking out toward some swampland.

Sticking his head and shoulders out the opened door, Mason called back, "What the hell are you looking for?"

"The dog. A dog. I heard a dog."

"There's no dog, Charles. Now get your fat ass back in here and let me tell you about my idea."

"There's a dog out there. Trust me."

"Okay, there's a dog out there. Somewhere. There's always a dog somewhere. What the hell does it matter? Get in here and let me tell you something."

Charlie took one more glance around and slid into the driver's seat. "Yeah, so what's your bright idea?"

"Well," Mason began, doing a drumroll on the metal dashboard, "first we get back to Fort Myers, get a room at a Motel 6 or something … and then hunt around Sanibel or Captiva the next day to rent for the season." He looked over with a big grin, but Charlie was squinting, glaring through the windshield far into the distance.

"Yeah, well, anyway … we call your" —air quotes— "responsible son Andrew and tell him to close up our houses for a few months, then rent a small place for the" —air quotes again—"season." Followed by an expanding grin, a gleaming grin, a gleaming grin full of anticipation.

For a moment Charlie wondered if this was Mason's seduction grin, but he shook that thought away. "Well, first, stop with the fucking air quotes—you sound like some Millennial twit from Brooklyn—and second, what's with those ridiculous white teeth? You get a new set of choppers?"

Mason exaggerated his smile. "Nice, hah? Got 'em capped." Then pointing at Charlie, "A helluva lot more attractive than those crooked yellow slabs of rotted wood filling your piehole."

"You're such a narcissist."

"And you're just figuring that out now?" He offered up another expanding, gleaming smile.

Then it sunk in. "The season?"

"Huh?"

"You said 'the season.' What season?"

"Spring training!" Mason yelped. "I just checked it out." He pointed to the phone. "Pitchers and Catchers is only like fifty-seven days away!"

But then Charlie was sliding out of the Jeep again, holding onto the steering wheel and standing on the loose gravel, pointing emphatically ahead. "You see that?"

"What?"

"That black dog wandering this way ... way out in the marsh."

"Oh Christ, I don't see anything. There's no dog out there. But what the hell do you think of my idea about spending the winter on Sanibel?"

Charlie's chest rose and fell before he urged himself through that veil. "Well, if we're gonna live together for a couple of months, there are a few things—maybe a few dozen things—we need to get straight."

**

Having successfully walked through that thin veil, and perhaps a few others over the next few hours on the drive south to Ft. Myers, Charlie told his old friend in a rambling monotone about the veil.

After a while Mason had to lean over to hear him say, "I can't really explain it, except to say that it is something I can see through, a thin curtain so unsubstantial, so porous, so easily brushed aside that I can't ever figure out how it has kept me contained in myself ... how it still keeps me from sharing an honest moment with the people I care about."

Mason was speechless. He just laid his palm on the back of his friend's warm neck as one might do to a child.

Charlie didn't move, both hands on the wheel, eyes on the road, his soft, gravelly voice continuing to speak from behind that veil: "I used to tell myself it got much worse—thicker, more opaque—after Joni died, but I now know that nothing changed when she died ... I just became more aware of it, more angry about it, how separate I was, always was, from Sarah and the kids, even Joni, who I thought walked on water ... who walked on water ..." His voice trailed off.

Now he turned to look at Mason, who first met his glance and then nodded, a smile flickering at the edges of his mouth. Charlie's lip began to tremble on its own until he could hardly catch his breath. "But I couldn't break through it. I couldn't do it. Ever." And a few seconds later: "And then I found that it's not just one veil, there are endless veils behind each veil."

Mason ordered him to pull the Jeep over to the side of the road. And rather than tell him to go fuck himself, as he might have done less than an hour before, Charlie wiped his eyes with the back of his hand, cupped the snot dripping out of his nose with his palm and wiped it on his shorts, then did as he was told. He even left the Jeep idling in neutral, saying, "Maybe you should drive."

When Mason got himself settled into the driver's seat, Charlie reached over, patted his knee, and, realizing he was back behind another veil, said, "And if that doesn't make you want to drop me off at the adult daycare center, let me tell you that was just a flimsy veil from this dimension. But I'm not ready to step through it right now, except to say"—he waited for Mason to look his way—"that the dog in the back seat is no hallucination."

Mason swung his head around, drifted into the middle lane, and saw an empty bench seat. "There's nothing there, Chuck."

"The blind shall receive sight, the lame walk, the lepers are cleansed, the deaf hear, the dead are raised, and the good news is preached to the poor."

"You're not getting religious on me, are you?"

"Luke 7:22. And fuck you," Charlie said out of the side of his mouth.

These were the last words the two of them spoke until Mason pulled into a weary looking Rodeway Inn outside Ft. Myers. He cut the engine, waited until the dieseling had stopped, and looked over. "And so, it begins all over again."

When Charlie nodded, he added, "Please leave the imaginary smelly dog in the car."

***

The next morning, after a mostly silent Febreze-filled night at the Rodeway, and a couple of Egg McMuffins and bitter coffee at the McDonald's drive-through, they crossed the bridge and stumbled upon a small frayed-at-the-edges cottage court on Sanibel's Jamaica Lane, Bougainvillea Cabins, a VACANCY sign surrounded by a pathetic-looking bougainvillea vine. Turned out that a seasonal renter had just died, so there was a cottage free through the middle of March.

Mason reached into his breast pocket and tossed a Visa card on Joe Fitzpatrick's messy desk, and less than two minutes later, the Osprey Cottage at the Bougainvillea Cabins was theirs until the middle of March.

Unpacking the Jeep took all of thirty seconds, and then Mason drove off to get some beer and cigarettes.

Which left Charlie alone, sitting on the screened porch with Sarus, elbows on the round table, smoking his last Lucky Strike. Halfway down the cigarette, he called Dylan.

Dylan was driving the Vanagon somewhere outside of Rocky Mount, North Carolina, with two other BadBreath-ers, heading down to gigs in Myrtle Beach and Charleston, then Beaufort, South Carolina, then St. Augustine, then Lauderdale, and finally Key West.

Dylan obviously didn't want to talk. He offered a lot of "sounds goods," some distracted sounding "yup, yup, yup"s, and, most amazing of all, no name calling before saying what he had wanted to say all along. "Listen, it's kinda hard talking right now. I'll call you tonight from Myrtle. In the meantime, please, please, please call my pain-in-my-ass brother and tell him what he needs to know so he can stop wringing his hands. Please ..."

121

Charlie agreed and, in a gesture probably equally amazing to both of them, restrained himself from agreeing that Andrew was indeed a pain in the ass. When he heard that insulting pop and the line went dead, right after thinking, *I'll go see him in Key West*, he speed-dialed Andrew:

"Dad."

"Hey ... this would be your pain-in-the-ass father."

"Are you home?"

'No, Florida."

"But I thought you and Mason—"

"Change in plans." And after dispensing a lot of reluctant information and even more back-and-forth about Cecilia and the kids missing him at Christmas, which Charlie knew was simply not true (except maybe for Cecilia), he answered some endless only-Andrew-would-ask questions ("Wait! Wait til I get a pad of paper") about mail, utilities, bills, the thermostat, snow plowing, suspending newspaper delivery, and on and on until Charlie blurted out, "I can't do this anymore, Andrew, it's giving me a headache. You do what you can and I'll call you tomorrow after I've had a six-pack and twenty or thirty cigarettes."

"Moderation, Dad."

"Thank you, son."

"And you know you shouldn't be smoking."

"Goodbye, Andrew. I love you." He pressed the End Call tab just as Andrew was saying, "I'll call you to—"

Charlie looked down at the dark screen on the phone, aching with biblical remorse.

***

It was to be a long night. Too much and not enough was said before Charlie started blubbering again. An embarrassment for both men. And then there was the lingering question of Sarus's presence.

After some quiet and increasingly easy smokes and beer on the screened porch at Osprey Cottage, followed by a silent walk down to the Gulf at the curved horseshoe end of Jamaica Lane, the two drove off for some shrimp at the Sunset Grille.

It was over Coronas at the Grille that Charlie broke the uneasy silence. "Remember I was talking about the veil?"

Mason lowered his face and looked over his glasses. "How could I forget? Tell you the truth, I wasn't going to mention it, hoping we didn't have to go back there."

"Well …," he went on as if there had been no irony involved in that exchange and proceeded to tell Mason about the *other* veil that he'd been walking through, the one from back at the hospital where he saw St. Augustine, Joni, and the dog, Sarus. And, although he hesitated before mentioning it, he also told Mason about the "visit" from Sarah.

Mason sat patiently and listened as his previously closed-mouth, grumbly old friend spoke in such an impassioned—and even reverent—way about overlapping dimensions of time and space, about the absurd notion of time being linear, and about the ludicrous idea of space being quantifiable. "I know you think I'm crazy—Andrew thinks I need to be locked up, and Sarah was right behind him before … you know—but I don't think I've ever been more sane."

"Well, that may be the first really, really, really crazy thing you've said." Mason leaned over the table and spoke just above a whisper. "You are a lunatic, my friend, you've always been two bricks short of a load, but it's got little to do with overlapping dimensions or that imaginary dog you think we got traveling with us."

"*Is* traveling with us."

Mason leaned back, picked up his bottle of beer, drained it, and said, "Have it your way. I don't see it."

"Joey saw it."

"Who the hell is Joey?"

"Kid on the Cape. Mother works at the lobster-roll stand in Sandwich. He saw the dog. Clear as day."

"So now you're seeing imaginary dogs *and* imaginary kids who see imaginary dogs? Okay, so now you're beginning to scare me. What's next? You gonna cut your nuts off, buy some new Nikes, and board the Hale Bop spaceship?"

Charlie stood then, tossed a twenty and then a ten on the table. "Let's get out of here. I can't talk to you about any of this anymore. I mean, you really are an idiot."

Mason took two twenties from his billfold, picked up the ten, and followed him out of the restaurant.

And the long journey into night got a lot longer.

Chapter Thirteen (or Four): November – March

That first night in the musty, frayed-at-every-one-of-the-edges Osprey Cottage, they consumed twelve bottles of Dos Equis, a half liter of Maker's Mark, two and a half packs of Luckies, and the handful of beef jerky that Mason picked up at the package store. By the time dawn bloodied the sky outside the screened porch, the two old college friends, roommated once again, had poured out more tightly held intimacies than they had ever before shared.

And by the time their confessions had made that predictable turn toward sloppy, drunken expressions of gratitude neither of them would remember or, if they did, repeat to anyone, Mason had laid bare his obvious-to-everyone-but-himself fear of communion with another soul, the shame of his serial cheating on one girlfriend after another, the desperate women he bedded and left behind on one cruise ship after another, one big band after another, the despair and humiliation of his current inability to "perform," his abiding fear of dying alone, and "the veil"—he pointed at Charlie—"I step through every time I pick up my trumpet and get lost in the notes." After a teary pause, eyes glistening, he added, "It's the only place I feel real." Then thirty seconds later, barely above a mumble, he also confessed his despair at "not having the guts to follow the music where it wanted to go. Bottom line, my friend: I am a hack."

And, in turn, never certain whether Mason could understand—or even hear—his new knowledge of space and time, Charlie poured out a litany of personal failures, every alternately enervating and invigorating thought rumbling through heart and head. That included the addled notion that St. Augustine and Joni and the hound were not illusions or delusions but actual presences who had led him to believe that "once we let go of the absurd notion that this"—he rapped his knuckles on the coffee table—"this"—then reached up and slapped his chest—"is the only reality"—he waited a few seconds until Mason was looking directly at him—"we can travel through space unfettered and unconstrained by the limitations of artificial time."

Mason nodded as if he heard it all, but Charlie noticed that his foot was bouncing up and down like he was distracted by the notes of some tune he might have been hearing inside his head.

Undeterred, Charlie forged headlong into a drunk and angry rambling reverie about the *Be Here Now* bullshit from Ram Dass and Robin Williams's carpe diem nonsense in *Dead Poets Society*, eventually contradicting himself by saying, "It's all true. It's all true ... we are alive only in the moment we are alive, no past, no future ... and yet"—he waved his finger in the air in front of the glazed-over Mason—"also alive in every moment, past and present, we've ever lived. It's body and soul, Mason, body and soul, they can't be separated. They just can't be separated. Ever."

And with that he ran out of steam and leaned back into the wicker couch, eyes closed, crickets buzzing all around.

In the long silence that followed, the rusted GE refrigerator inside the cottage adding to the hum in the background, Charlie was back to thinking about the fact that the kid Joey had actually seen the dog. A half hour later, seemingly out of nowhere, he said, "The kid really did see the dog, Mason.

126

There's no making that up." And a few moments after that he added, "I understand the concept of parallel universes, but I just can't figure out how to move between them or how to call any of them up again … I mean, how do I walk through the veil from one dimension to another?"

"I don't know what to say."

"You and Dylan."

The sky over the little cottage was now turning blue, the ground still shaded by the evening darkness like a Magritte painting. "Well, maybe there's nothing more to say," Charlie said and got up and lumbered back to the tiny bedroom behind the kitchen. And after closing the door, unbuttoning and dropping his old Wrangler cutoffs on the floor, and sitting down on the bed, he shrugged and said, "Maybe we said it all. What the hell else is there to say?"

It seemed too exhausting then to brush his teeth, so he swiveled around, lay down on the mushy pillow, and spoke to the spots of mold on the ceiling: "I mean, after all is said and done, Sarah's dead … and why the hell does any of this really matter?"

***

They both awakened a few hours later grumpy and hungover and, like the moaning college roommates they once were, promising never to abuse their bodies again.

And from that moment forward neither of them mentioned anything about empty hookups or co-opted art or lost opportunities or parallel universes … or anything remotely intimate.

Instead, the two old friends quickly became something of an old married couple, two hunched-over old men silently walking the beach each morning in their cut-off jeans, clunky white sneakers, and black socks, hands clasped behind their backs, their unleashed dog waddling and meandering in the dune grasses. In the afternoons they'd ride the rental bikes up to Captiva or over to Ding Darling, occasionally heading into Ft. Myers to catch an Indians or Red Sox Grapefruit League game. Then showers before heading off to early-bird specials at Timbers or Cips, followed by quiet and even quieter nights reading books brought back from the library on Dunlop Road.

Charlie did not take a photograph the entire time the two of them were on the island, grumbling every time they passed a gallery with bird and dune photographs in the window. And although he continued to see Mason's knee bouncing up and down in various cadences he was obviously hearing in his head, Mason had left his trumpet back home—and the local music scene was, as Mason scoffed, "such fucking suburban shtick" that he refused to turn on the radio.

So, there was no art and no music in their shared Sanibel lives until Charlie received a hurried call from Dylan near the end of February saying that BadBreath's gig at Blue Heaven in Key West was coming up. Abandoning their morning routine (coffee, walk on the beach, Mason making breakfast ["because Sarah treated you like a child, and you never learned to cook or take care of yourself"], Charlie straightening up the cottage ["because you're a fucking pig"]) the two left Sanibel early the next morning, got some breakfast at the Lighthouse Café, and drove across Alligator Alley, through Homestead and then on down US 1 to the Keys.

During the near-silent drive, road noise and cracked muffler filling every blank space, Mason, who had played on many cruises that docked at Key West, called ahead and booked a couple of rooms at the Coco Plum Inn on Whitehead St. and made 7 p.m. reservations for two near the stage at Blue Heaven.

Arriving at the inn late in the afternoon, Charlie stood back, feeling that old discomforting sense of separation as Mason was greeted so warmly by Joanna Payne and Jim

FitzPatrick, former big band members on the early Born at the Wrong Time tours, now the proprietors of the inn.

After introductions were made and they were shown their rooms, Mason started acting awkward in a way that Charlie had never witnessed before, refusing the Joanna's invitation for drinks around the pool, saying he wanted to show Charlie the Audubon House. He pointed up Whitehead as if they didn't know where it was.

He acted odd, seemingly ponderous, on the way there, too. And when they learned from the young and pretty docent that recent research had determined that John James Audubon had never actually lived there, just visited a few times, Mason didn't say a word. He remained silent even when Charlie refused to pay the fourteen-dollar admission, muttering "This is bullshit" and walking out, holding the door open for Sarus.

Out on the street, Mason finally spoke: "Y'know, you really are the same jackass you were way back in Williamstown. You may be walking through any number of veils or membranes or whatever the hell you want to call your invisible shields these days—but inside you're still the same old self-righteous jackass I've always known."

Charlie glared at him and was just about to shoot back and call him whatever crude expression would have once so easily spewed out of his mouth, but now, it seemed, he could not evade the simple truth of Mason's ire. "Yep. I am." And a few seconds after that, "You too."

Now it seemed to be Mason's turn to ponder that simple truth.

Charlie patted his friend's shoulder, saying, "Well, let's the two of us jackasses go over to Hemingway's pile," and quickly adding, "He actually did live there."

They walked shoulder to shoulder the other way on Whitehead and were just passing the Coco Plum when Charlie asked, seemingly out of nowhere, "Hey, did you and Joanna have a thing?"

Mason didn't look at Charlie, just kept walking—and staring—ahead. "No" was all he said.

Charlie knew he was lying, but saw no reason to challenge him just then. And when they arrived at the Hemingway house and found that the joint had closed at 4:30, they turned around without a word or a curse and the two old men lumbered back toward the Coco Plum.

Before they turned to open the gate, though, Mason stopped, glared at Charlie, and said, "She wasn't interested."

Charlie laughed, a smoker's laugh, and then instantly felt sorry. "I wasn't judging, just beginning to figure some things out for myself. Sorry."

"That 'sorry,'" Mason said, "may be the scariest word of the day—and the idea of you figuring out anything may be the scariest moment of this entire ridiculous adventure down here."

Charlie didn't answer; walked onto the property, through the second gate, alongside the pool, and up the four steps to the narrow porch; and disappeared into his room. Stepped up on the riser and lay down on the too-tall bed. And as had become routine since Sarah died, he stared up at the ceiling until everything disappeared in the plaster swirls or mildew dots or water stains.

A couple of hours later he was awakened out of a frustrating dream of making a frame for a photograph by someone knocking on his door. "Wake up, you old coot!" Mason.

"Door's open—" he called, stopping himself from saying "asshole."

The door swung open, and Mason appeared like a gunslinger in a grade B western, standing there in the portal, surrounded by the white frame, pool visible behind him. "She was the one," he said.

"The one?"

Mason lowered his eyes. "I think so."

"You think so?"

He nodded.

Charlie swung his feet off the bed and toed around for the step stool. "Well, doesn't that just sum it all up? How many other 'ones' were there before and after she showed you the door?"

"A few," he said. And a few seconds later he added, "But she was nothing like the others."

Charlie smirked. "Oh, really?"

Mason glared as if he might draw a gun or leap across the space and strangle him. But he just muttered, "You're a piece of crap, Charlie Messina."

"I am."

And with that resolved, the two wandered over to the Blue Heaven on Thomas Street to eat and catch Dylan and the rest of BadBreath doing the first of their three sets. They stayed until the place closed at 11 p.m.

Charlie figured they'd hang out with Dylan then—and maybe grab some breakfast at La Crêperie before heading back to Sanibel the next morning. But as it turned out, BadBreath was booked in South Beach the next night, so the band packed up right after their last song.

Although he told Dylan how disappointed he was that the band had to get on the road right away, he was privately relieved Dylan was leaving. With Mason, at least, he didn't have to rise to any occasion. Dylan provided his own veil.

Leaving the rest of the band behind to load up the RV, the three of them walked to Dylan's van parked on Emma Street. Charlie embraced Dylan. Gave him a quick kiss on the hairy cheek. Promised to get together again soon. And when the

Vanagon pulled out, engine pinging, into the warm night, making a right and disappearing up Petronia Street, Charlie noticed the achingly sad expression on his old friend's face. "The only one?"

"I think so." Mason sat down on a nearby bench, leaned elbows on his knees, and lowered his head. "Go on"—he waved—"I'll meet you back there."

With Sarus heeling the whole way, Charlie left Mason likely brooding about wasting his life playing cruise ships and bedding rich widows, and walked back to the Coco Plum, brooding to himself about all the lost time he'd spent behind one veil or another.

***

Back on Sanibel there was more of the same: the beach walks, the bike rides, Ding Darling, early bird specials, and for Charlie, a weekly call from Andrew, where he tried his best to assure his son that he was fine, asking the same three questions of his grandchildren (How's school? How's soccer/gymnastics/music lessons/basketball? What would you like me to bring you back from Florida?), his hunched shoulders relaxing when Cecilia would get on the phone and he'd guffaw and cough, cough over her stories of life with her "sweet, lovable, anal-retentive Andrew and his anal-retentive spawn" back in Rhode Island.

Mason received no calls. Never asked what Charlie talked about with the family, as Sarah always had. Never seemed to call anyone, although Charlie found him sitting in the Jeep one afternoon on his cell phone.

"Who were you talking to?" he asked later.

Mason seemed surprised, eyebrows shooting up. "No one, just some, y'know ..." He didn't finish. Charlie wondered if it could have been Joanna from the Coco Plum, but he didn't ask.

***

Mason never once saw Sarus, but soon enough he stopped trying to tell Charlie he wasn't there. And when he spotted Charlie sitting out on the screened porch, lips moving, he no longer asked who was in the room with him.

It was an easy life, certainly a respite from the cold wind and snow around Newport, a respite from the hard questions, all questions being hard at that point. And that was fine. Enough. Or at least just enough.

But all that changed on March 15, when the Osprey Cottage rental ended and they tossed their satchels in the back of the Jeep to head home. Pretty much a straight shot up 75 to the ugliest road in America, I-95, a night in Jacksonville, another night outside of Rocky Mount, and, the old Jeep engine straining the entire way, another long, boring day and night landed them right back in Newport.

If anyone was monitoring the ride, it might have seemed remarkable how little the two men talked the entire 1,500 miles. For three days it seemed that although they were only traveling major highways, each was locked in the back roads of his own memories and some fearful understanding of what lay ahead as those roads got smaller and smaller. At 7 p.m. on March 18, Charlie dropped off Mason at his condo and then slowly, barely making the speed limit, headed over to 17 Ledge Road, where he found the lights on and Andrew's SUV in the driveway.

He pulled into the garage, saw Sarah's Toyota right where he'd left it, doused the lights, killed the engine, and then sat there breathing in and out through his nose until his heart stopped thudding. Then reached into the glove box and found the last cigarette in the pack. Lit it. Took a deep inhale. Blew it out in a long silver stream. Plucked a piece of tobacco off his tongue. Took one more toke and threw the butt on the garage floor. Mushed it when he got out of the Jeep.

As he walked out of the garage, the motion sensor lights instantly lit up the breezeway, and, as if no time had passed, there were Andrew, Cecilia, and the two kids standing—each of them beaming—behind the glass storm door. It was freezing. March 18, in Newport, Rhode Island.

The last place on earth Charlie Messina wanted to be.

***

Weeks later, Charlie had settled into a routine that, if little else, kept his mind off the loneliness, the coldness in the empty house that each night burrowed all the way down into his bones. Waking just after dawn each day, driving downtown, having breakfast (coffee, two eggs over easy, home fries) at the Corner Café on Broadway, going home, firing up the gas fireplace in the studio, and going to work on the series of prints of Joey and Manny. As before, as ever, somehow he knew that those portraits were the essence of his current project, looking more and more like a final project. And the knowledge that there was something akin to salvation or wisdom or maybe even peace in seeing it through to its end.

But right then he couldn't see the meaning behind the project, couldn't imagine it, couldn't step into each moment of it with any confidence that he wouldn't be walking off a cliff. Another paper bag he couldn't punch his way through; another veil he couldn't navigate.

Nevertheless, that daily routine invariably brought him right into the early afternoon where, sapped by his endless obsession with the veils and the daily demands of the dark room, wandering blindly, haltingly, down a dark hall, one hand scraping along a wall, toeing tentatively into each next step, he would arrive in the kitchen to either cut off a slab of cheddar cheese and roll up two or three slices of salami or skip lunch altogether, either way collapsing afterward on the living room couch for an hour's nap.

134

By then it would be 3 p.m., time to bundle up, rouse Sarus, get in the Jeep, light up a Lucky, drive down Ruggles Road, get out, and do the Cliff Walk, rain or shine, taking some time every day to wander the Salve Regina campus. If he walked slowly enough, and had a good tune in his head to override thoughts of Sarah and Joni (he still refused to walk around like some fool with earbuds in his ears), he'd get back to the Jeep by 5:30, just in time to drive over to Andrew and Cecilia's, where he'd been coerced into being a nightly dinner guest in exchange for Saturday night babysitting ... and, just as important, Andrew's promise that he would never stick him in St. Clare's when Charlie became totally daft. (Daft was Andrew's word, not his. He'd said something about shitting in his pants.)

All of which was good enough for the time until one Saturday early in mid-April when Charlie was babysitting Jack and Diane. Jack got up from watching TV and, maybe hearing something, looked out the front window and gasped, "You got a dog sitting in your Jeep, Pop!"

Charlie hadn't moved that fast since he had been stung by a wasp one day on Sanibel. He parted the curtains. There was Sarus, sitting on the passenger seat, just where he had left him.

"A dog, D-O-G?"

Jack looked at Charlie like he was daft, like Andrew often looked at him. "Course I see him—he's right there," he whispered, pointing out toward the Jeep. "Just don't tell Diane, she'll freak."

But the warning came too late. Diane had heard the commotion and the word "dog," and ran in from the playroom. "What dog? What dog?" she cried, desperately afraid of all dogs.

"Out there in Pop's Jeep," Jack told her in a voice that sounded like a docent or a hall monitor.

She ran behind Charlie, wrapped her arms around his knee, and when he parted the curtain, she sidled very slowly around in front of him.

"You see him in the front seat?"

Holding tightly on to his thigh, Diane pressed her nose to the window, looked and looked, wiped away her breath, and looked again. Shook her head.

He turned to Jack. "You still see him?"

"Yep. Right there," he said, his finger pressed to the glass.

"I don't see anything," Diane said.

"Must be the angle you're looking from," Charlie said and closed the curtain. Then turning to Jack: "Let's just let him stay there."

"But it's cold," Jack said.

Charlie shrugged and closed the curtain. "Looks like he's got a thick coat," he said, falling back into the couch with a smile spreading across his unshaven mug, thinking Jack had to meet Joey sometime. There was work to be done.

He picked up the still-anxious Diane and plopped her down on his lap. "You know, sweet girl, ol' Pop isn't crazy after all."

***

First things first, though. Sunday morning, right after eggs and coffee at the Corner Café, Charlie and Sarus drove over to the Sunoco.

By this time, Sarus was no longer just appearing and disappearing at whim (his whim), but was pretty much a constant companion wherever Charlie went ... curled up in the tattered passenger seat of the Jeep, under the drafting table, on the couch (completely contrary to Sarah's rule about a dog's place in the home), on Sarah's empty side of the bed (ditto).

Charlie pulled into the station and parked next to the convenience store window so that the passenger seat was right across the sidewalk from the cash register, making sure Manny was behind the counter.

He was watching the TV hung on the wall over the display of chips. His eyes widened, as they always did whenever Charlie lumbered into the shop. Charlie put his hands in the air as a promise he'd behave himself. But this time Manny seemed to relax, to continue breathing, color coming back to his face.

Right. The garage was closed on Sundays.

Not that Manny looked so comfortable, his shoulders up near his ears as Charlie took the one, two, three steps to the counter.

"So, kid, looks like we can exchange pleasantries and I can procure myself a pack of Luckies without getting my nose rearranged. Hah?" And with no other mask to offer, he coughed and watched as Manny, without looking at him and without a word, reached up a skinny arm to pluck out a pack of Lucky Strikes off the rack, and with the other, fished a pack of matches out of the box next to the cash register.

Did a smirk squiggle out of Manny's lips as he said, "That'll be twelve dollars"?

Charlie already had the cash in his fist. Looking the kid right in the eye, he slid the money across the counter with one hand and with the other slid the pack of cigarettes and matches back his way.

Which was when Manny started to say his usual "Have a good one," but Charlie cut him off. "Since we have this rare opportunity to speak without the threat of violence, I just have one question for you."

Manny's eyes grew wide again.

"It's not a trick question—and it's not going to get you in trouble with your old man."

Manny nodded, still wide-eyed, still looking around for his absent father to appear. "All I want you to do," Charlie went on, "is look out that window and let me know if you see a dog sitting in my Jeep. That's all I'm asking."

Manny nodded again, turned to the window, and then glanced back, now appearing a bit catatonic. "Relax, Manny, this is not a test. No one's gonna yell at you or hit you if you get the wrong answer. In fact, there is no right answer. All I want to know is if you see a dog sitting on the seat."

Manny nodded again.

"Take a breath, son, oxygenate your brain, and use your words. Do you see a dog in the Jeep?"

Manny opened his mouth and a second or two later, pressed out his lips and whispered, "No."

"Okay! Now a harder question: If I did have a dog, what color do you suppose it would be?"

Manny turned back toward the window and then, even more quietly, said, "Black?"

"Hmmmm. Well, maybe now we're getting somewhere. Thank you. Thank you very much." He reached across the counter offering a handshake. Manny glanced over Charlie's shoulder—likely just to make sure no one was in the bays— and took his hand. Shook it once, firmly, probably like he had been told, and then attempted to pull his hand back. But Charlie tightened his grasp. "Now just one more question, an easy one: How old are you?"

"Fifteen?"

"Well, I don't know, Manny," Charlie said and laughed, "fifteen looks right, but you probably know it better than I. Let's just agree that you're fifteen." He reached over the counter with his other hand and patted the back of Manny's girlishly soft hand. "Thank you, my young friend."

Then let go. Manny didn't move. Just stared—wide-eyed again—across the counter. "Have a good one," he said.

Charlie smiled back, bursting with affection for the boy. "One? Is that all? Just one measly one? What would happen if I asked for more than one?"

"It's just a—"

"Well, it's a lot more than *just* anything. Don't sell yourself short. I say go out there and get yourself a couple, maybe three or four. Then we'll meet up sometime and compare ones."

And with that bit of confounding nonsensical advice, he gave the kid a thumbs up, turned, walked jauntily out of the shop and around the back of the rumbling Jeep, sliding into the driver's seat almost like the young man he once was. Then patted Sarus's shoulder, caressed his ear before taking the new pack of cigarettes from his coat pocket, pulling the red cellophane tag, ripping the metallic paper, slapping the pack against his open palm, and wrapping his lips around the one cigarette that pushed ahead. He drove out of the gas station, happier and more carefree than he'd been in a long, long time. Maybe since he'd been named All-Conference Linebacker for the Jonathon Law Eagles in Milford.

Two blocks later, unlit cigarette in his mouth, he dug deep in his Members Only jacket pocket to find the matches, then took both hands off the steering wheel, struck the match, and lit the cigarette. A big inhale and a silent exhaling ahhh brought him to heart-thudding red brake lights—and the neck-jarring bumper of a rusted, beat-up F-150 Ford pickup.

Esmerelda Santiago pulled over onto the shoulder, then waited as Charlie bang-bang-banged his fist on the steering wheel, took another long toke on the cigarette, drove off onto the shoulder and urged himself out the door. Flicking the half-smoked cigarette to the pavement, he walked around the front of the Jeep, bent down to examine the indented bumper, and then pivoted to confirm that was exactly where he had run into her hitch. It was hard to tell if the battered truck had suffered any damage.

Making his way slowly around to the driver's side of the truck—the driver had still not gotten out—Charlie had not decided whether he was going to be charming and apologetic or irate that the fool had jammed on the brakes. But when he glared up into the eyes of Ms. Santiago, a strikingly sad woman who could have been thirty or fifty, he saw clearly at least a dozen different truths—all the same one—about her life and quickly dropped all the theater going on in his head. "No damage," he said, shaking his head. "Just a small dent in my old piece-of-crap Jeep bumper. Your truck looks fine. It was all my fault."

He held out his hand. "Charlie Messina."

Hesitant at first, Ms. Santiago didn't say a word but extended her own small, rough palm.

And that would have been the uneventful end of their chance meeting if she had not held on to Charlie's hand a beat too long and then, looking behind her, asked, *"Esta bien tu perro?"*

He was confused. Pressed his lips together and wagged his head. *"No habla ..."*

Taking her hand back, the woman pointed her thumb behind her. "Woof woof?"

Still confused, he shrugged.

"Mmm ... jur perrito ... ahhh, hmmm, puppy?"

For a second, with the traffic behind him and the clouds swirling in the sky above the trees, he grew dizzy.

"Puppy, si?"

"You can see the dog?"

Ms. Santiago looked blank. First pointing two fingers at his eyes and then turning them around her way, he said, "You can see the puppy?"

The woman smiled, showing two teeth missing up top. "Si! *Perro negro. Esta bien?"*

To which he responded with the entirety of his Spanish vocabulary. *"Si. Bueno. Gracias!"* And then added most unexpectedly, *"Que tengas un buen día,"* although he hadn't spoken a sentence of Spanish since Spanish Conversation class at Williams—and wasn't at all sure how that phrase came out of his mouth.

And with that bit of pleasantries taken care of, Esmerelda Santiago uttered several *Gracias*-es and drove out of his life. Charlie got back into the Jeep with Sarus, patted the dog's rump, lit up another cigarette, and said, "Well, ain't that a hoot."

Sarus looked up, which Charlie realized had never happened before, and wagged his tail. For a few seconds Charlie waited breathlessly, thinking the hound might actually say something, but when no words were spoken, he took one drag, then another, before mumbling, "That certainly upsets the old apple cart, doesn't it? Practically everything I was beginning to think is true is maybe flat-out wrong."

And that was before a Newport cop, looking more like a female Naval officer than a local cop, pulled up behind the Jeep, lights flashing. He came to the door and asked, "You all right, Charlie?"

"Fine. Just had a little fender bender—nothing to report."

"Do you know where you are, Charlie?"

"Of course, I know where I am."

"Where are we, Charlie?"

"How the hell do you know my name? I didn't give you my license." Now things were beginning to feel really weird. The sun streaked through the windshield.

"The dog," the cop said. "What about the dog?"

"You see the dog?"

PART IV.I

"Just as real events are forgotten, some that never were can be in our memories as if they happened."

— Gabriel García Márquez, *Memories of My Melancholy Whores*

Chapter Fourteen (or One), August Sometime

"You see the dog?" you repeated with some urgency through the darkness.

"Charlie?"

The voice sounded like Sarah, but you knew it couldn't be her. You knew Sarah's voice. Your eyes fluttered against the glaring light and you clamped them shut.

"Oh, Cecilia, oh my God," you heard from far away, "I think he's waking up! I think he's waking up." Then you felt Sarah's soft and warm fingers, her ring, her ring! "Charlie, it's me! Open your eyes."

Then, moments later, maybe months later, someone else without soft fingers presses against your eye, pushing your eyelid up, shining a flashlight. You clamped your eye shut. "What the hell are you doing?"

"Charlie," a man's voice says. "Open your eyes."

You lifted your eyelids to see blurry faces all around. "What is this?" you had to force out of your dry throat. "Where am I? Where is Sarah? Am I dead?"

The faces in front of the light gaining some clarity, laughing. "No! You're alive!" That one sounded like Cecilia.

Fuzzy shapes hardened into focus. It was Cecilia.

Next to her … Sarah. "Sarah?" you stuttered. "Is that you? I am dead, right?"

She was crying and laughing. "No, I mean yes, it's me—and no, you're not dead, you old goat!" You felt her lips on the back of your hand. For real.

"You've been … unconscious … in a coma, Charlie, but—"

You clenched your eyes shut again and opened them. "How long have I been out? Where is the cop? I was just talking to the cop."

You could see Sarah, dead or alive, glancing over at Andrew. Andrew! Andrew looked at his watch. "Almost three days," he said. "What cop, Dad?"

"Welcome back," the guy who looked like a doctor said.

"But where's the dog?"

"What dog?" Sarah asked and shrugged.

"The dog, Sarus, you know."

"BadBreath?" she asked, obviously confused, glancing over at the doctor. "BadBreath died quite a while ago, Charlie. Don't you remember?"

"Of course, I remember! I'm talking about Sarus. And what about Esmerelda Santiago? She didn't get deported, did she?"

"Who?"

***

Sarah, Andrew, Cecilia, Dylan, and Mason (who showed up a few hours later) all desperately tried every which way—and sideways—to convince you that you had only been unconscious for two days. "Two and a half days," said Andrew.

"And no one's dead, sweetheart. I'm right here," said Sarah.

"She's right here, Dad."

And then, through the next unbelievably confusing few hours, you found out that you had *not* been traveling ... to Northampton with Dylan ... or to Madison, Wisconsin with BadBreath ... or to Sanibel Island with Mason.

"Of course, I was," you growled, glaring at them one by one, the light outside growing dim. And then, calendar days behind your eyes fluttering backward, you asked, "What about the whole rigmarole with St. Augustine? And Joni? And the damn dog?"

Following a few moments of silence during which many sets of eyes darted around the room, there was Sarah again: "It was just a dream, Charlie. You were unconscious, sweetheart."

"The hell I was."

Then it was Andrew's turn: "You were in a coma, Dad. You've been here the whole time. We've all been here the whole time. Just two and a half days. Not anywhere else. Right here ..." His voice trailed off.

In the hushed silence that followed, the lamp turned on as you looked around at each face again, each one growing more clear, each face wracked with consternation, until Sarah spoke once more: "I don't know, Charlie. I don't know." She picked up your hand again, but you brushed her away. "I don't know what you're talking about. You do know that Joni died?"

"Of course, I do! Jesus Christ, I'm not an imbecile."

"So ... what are you trying to tell us?"

"I'm not trying to tell you anything. I'm telling you I saw Joni. I saw St. Augustine when this whole thing began. I'm telling you I already told you all that. And I'm telling you I traveled all over fucking creation with a dog named Dumbass"—stopping momentarily to look into Sarah's eyes—"who I renamed Sarus after, well ... you died."

"I didn't die, Charlie," she said, eyes pooling again. "I'm right here. With you. I've been here the whole time."

"You died. You just don't know it."

"Charlie!"

"Don't 'Charlie' me. I know what I know."

Dylan put his hand on your shoulder. "Dad—"

"And don't you 'Dad' me." You inhaled through your nose, held the breath, and glared all around the hospital room. Then you turned on your side, away from the family.

Behind you, a man's voice, maybe the doctor, said something like, "Let's give him a little space and—"

Sarah cut him off: "I'm not leaving." You felt her arm reaching across your side. This time you let her.

"But I don't want to talk," you mumbled into the pillow. "I've apparently got some thinking to do."

***

Dark-haired, lithe, and stunning in that sexless manner of so many middle-aged medical professionals holding metal clipboards, Dr. Fishman-Fieldston smiled warmly and introduced herself as a member of the Post-Trauma Team.

You sat up. "Post-Trauma Team, huh? What position do you play?"

When she didn't answer immediately, you offered, "I'm thinking cornerback ... thin, fast, the last line of defense once the receiver has hit open field."

She smiled again. This time, though, she seemed actually amused. You detected a hint of her humanity at the corners of those thin painted lips. "Very good, Mr."—she looked down at the chart—"Messina. I guess I would think of myself more as a safety, but my husband might—"

"Well done, doctor," you said, cutting her off. "So ... what do you think of the Pats' chances this year? Y'think there will be a new pretty boy prancing around in the backfield?"

She tilted her head and pressed her lips together. "Well, I have no idea about Bill Belichick's plans, but"—she flipped one, then two pages up over the top of the metal case—"you have already answered the first two pages of my questionnaire."

"Good!"

"Well, actually very good."

"So ..." You lowered your black plastic Rite-Aid reading glasses for effect and looked up into the doctor's green eyes. She didn't look away.

"So?"

"So, I'm thinking you think I'm crazy. Or at least my entire family thinks I'm crazy, and they want you to check up on me. You know, wires crossed upstairs? Dementia? Another seventy-five-year-old dribbling and drooling candidate for the funny farm?"

She laughed. "No, no, no, no, Mr. Messina, I'm really here to help you transition out of the hospital." She pointed an index finger to the badge on her white jacket.

DR. FISHMAN-FIELDSTON, GERIATRIC PSYCHIATRY

"What they call an Exit Evaluation to help ensure that your next steps will be the right ones for you."

You burst out in a smoker's laughter. "Wow! First, that's at least two too many 'no's for me to trust your denials. And that little riff sounded just like the post-office lady going on postal autopilot … 'Is there anything liquid, fragile, perishable, or potentially hazardous, blah blah blah.'"

Dr. Fishman-Fieldston shook her head and flattened out what seemed to be a flowering toothy smile. "Got me." She flipped up another page of her questionnaire. "And got yourself another page closer to getting rid of me."

"Now we're talking," tilting your head in what you had always thought was a disarming pose. "Are you breaking up with me?"

Her flirty countenance changed. Became a bit flinty. "Well, that is the purpose of these things, isn't it?" And with that she closed the metal case and went on with her professional voice: "There is one thing I'd like to discuss with you, though, Mr. Messina."

You consciously arched your thick eyebrows.

"Would you tell me a little about seeing St. Augustine and your daughter"—she opened the metal case again, scanning the chart—"Joni? And what about the dog? Is he still around? Do you know where he is?"

A scowl crossed your face. "Oh Christ, you too! Don't you also want to know about the trip to Sanibel?"

Her face lost the rest of its brightness as she inhaled through her nose and didn't seem to let the breath go. "If you'd like to share that with me, Charlie, I'd be happy to hear about it all."

"Okay," you said, nodding, pressing your lips together, "I got it. I'm finally beginning to understand."

"Good." She smiled. A kindergarten teacher's smile. "Tell me what do you think happened."

You closed your eyes. And when you finally opened them again, you said, "I'll tell you everything in a minute. But first, you tell me what you understand about parallel universes ... about time—" You paused then, searching for the right word.

"Travel?" she said brightly.

"No! I'm not talking about Jules Verne; I'm talking about the limits of linear time."

The doctor seemed at first stunned by the force of your voice, looking unbalanced like she might topple over, but then she apparently found her footing and smiled the thin professional smile you had first seen a few minutes before. "I'm a scientist, Mr. Messina. I try to stay away from science fiction."

That required a nod. "Okay. Now I really do get it, Dr. Fishman-Fieldston. What do you want me to tell you about Joni and the dog?"

***

Three days later, you'd been back in the house on Ledge Road for two days, and Sarah was out at the Stop & Shop. You were sitting alone on the metal stool in the studio, arranging and rearranging dozens of photos of the two boys, Joey and Manny, who you were still sure held the keys to understanding where you'd been—and if not that, at least the essence of your next and final project.

Every so often you reached down, hoping to find Sarus (or Dumbass or whatever the dog's name was then), that block head and floppy ears, but the damn dog was nowhere to be found.

Nor were the words to explain to your wife and sons—or that jackass Mason—all the places you'd been to, the veils you'd stepped through. But they—all of them—kept insisting you'd been "out" just a little over sixty hours.

You glanced down at the shot of Manny's old man holding a tire iron over his head and instantly understood four things:

1.No one who mattered—and who was not insane—would ever believe your story.

2.You were a step or two away from your horrified family dumping you at St. Clare's.

3.Existence is not linear. There are overlapping times and dimensions, veils to break through, checkpoints to pass, that do not correspond to neat constructs by small-minded philosophers and psychologists and scientists, not to mention one's wife and children, who insist and insist and insist and goddamn insist that the universe is a series of causes and effects, equal and opposite actions and reactions ... yadda, yadda, yadda ... and fucking yadda.

4.And maybe most important, sixty hours in one context could be two months or two years or two centuries in another. It's all about where you're looking at time—and what kind of wide-angle lens you happen to be looking through. "Think *Inherit the Wind,*" you said out loud. No one answered.

And thus you promised yourself to never again mention anything that had happened during your recent, for lack of a better description, time travel. And that you would be nicer ... kinder ... sweeter to your sweetheart, Sarah, who didn't deserve everything you'd put her through in all the years since Joni died.

Then, seemingly out of nowhere, though you were quite sure than nothing came out of nowhere, you were thinking about Wallace Stevens's brilliant poem "The Snowman," which you had not thought about or understood since Joni showed it to you so excitedly on a break from her studies in Chapel Hill. So, you Googled the poem:

"the sound of the land
Full of the same wind
That is blowing in the same bare place

For the listener, who listens in the snow,
And, nothing himself, beholds
Nothing that is not there and the nothing that is."

And with a grunt you stood up and lumbered over to the bookshelves in the den. The slim volume was still there, and you index fingered it off the shelf, bringing it to your nose, thinking you might smell her on the pages.

There was no trace of Joni around, but you felt almost instantly better, a message from somewhere, a confirmation that you were not completely lost in forgetfulness, a doddering old fool, *a tattered coat upon a stick.*

And when Sarah returned with an armload of groceries, you were waiting for her in the kitchen with a heart full of love, smiling at the sight of your ever-gorgeous wife, not to mention the Pepperidge Farm Mint Milanos on the top of one of the bags, and after kissing her long and lustily, you told her you'd get the rest of the groceries out of the car.

"What was that all about?" she asked when you returned, arms full of three bags, and dumped them on the counter. "Not that I'm complaining," she added with a girlish smile.

"It's about finally understanding some things."

"Understanding what?" She stood stiffly right there in the kitchen, glaring at you. "I'm frankly not understanding much of what you're saying these days."

You laughed and opened your arms wide, taking a step toward her, but Sarah held up her palm like a cop. "Wait right there, mister. What exactly are you understanding? You worry me, Charlie Messina."

Stopped midstride, you said, "I know." Then looking down at the oak floor like a little boy, "And I'm sorry. I am just beginning to get a hold on what happened to me when I was in a coma."

"For two and a half days?"

"Yes, dear woman, for two and a half days, yes. I am very clear on that now. Very much so." You followed it with a sweet smile. Maybe genuine.

She smiled back, worry still spreading across her lined face like cracks forming in alabaster as you crossed the kitchen and wrapped your arms around the love of your life. Spoke into the comforting scent of her silver hair: "I have just come to see that the mind is a marvelous instrument, one that allows someone to recreate the illusions of time and space."

"Really?" she whispered into your shoulder.

"Really."

Then there was tea, the two Milanos you were allowed, sitting quietly and patiently, listening to Sarah talk, eyes glistening, about how terrible the ordeal had been when you were in the hospital, how frightened and lost she had felt.

And when she was spent, looking like she'd aged ten years, she walked into the living room to disappear into her book. You went out to the garage to sneak a cigarette ... later tiptoeing back into the studio, sitting on the comfortably uncomfortable metal swivel stool, reaching down to find Dumbass's block head and floppy ears.

You'd already known he'd be there.

And you knew then, finally, the journey was actually just beginning all over again.

PART IV.II

"This moment, this instant is important, not some unknown time in the future. Today, this very day, is what matters. We must put our entire beings into the present - for future victory is contained in this moment."

— Daisaku Ikeda, *The Wisdom for Creating Happiness and Peace*, Chap. 5.4.

Chapter Fifteen (or Two or One): July Redux

You think it's like some kind of déjà vu, but of course it isn't. And it's not some idiotic Hollywood science fiction film about time machines. It's something else. It's tectonic, ever-shifting plates within the geology of a planet that feels stationary but is traveling 66,700 miles an hour around the sun. And what's more, you're now beginning to see that every static, rock-solid moment repeats itself again and again and even amends itself in endlessly subtle ways each time you enter a new strata. But in the end, which is never ending, the experience is always the same.

And then you're humming that previously laughable tune from "Fiddler on the Roof."

Nevertheless, you're on the road again. You pop the clutch and make a right toward the village of Newport. Press the iPod plugged into the cigarette lighter, try yowling "Freedom!" along with Richie Havens for a couple of beats, but give up, no closer to the freedom you know is waiting for you just on the other side. "All you have to do is drive into and through it, old man," you say so familiarly, braking hard at the light.

Although you know in something akin to mental muscle memory that you aren't going on errands this time, right now you still aren't sure why you're headed this way. That's the way this seems to go. But when the light turns green, you drive right past the post office, then the frame shop, then the hospital; signal a right on Broadway; and are soon headed out of town on 138, roaring past the Lowe's and moving right along as the old Jeep rumbles through Fall River.

New Bedford.

Wareham.

In Sandwich you spot Gertie's Roadside Rest up ahead and pull into the gravel lot. The kid isn't around. You leave Dumbass in the Jeep, walk stiffly up to the window, and order a lobster roll and a Coke from the kid's mother. She smiles but does not recognize you. Of course. Though you do wonder. Then you walk back to the parking lot, boost yourself up on the warm hood, and breathe in the summer breeze on the Cape, which, as you have always told yourself, feels fresher than the marshy air around Newport.

With a mouthful of lobster meat, you mutter, "Just have some goddamn faith. You've already walked through three-four-five veils or cauls or membranes or whatever the goddamn hell they are. Maybe more."

"What?" comes a young, girly voice off to the side. Joey. Sitting on the banana seat of his bike. "I thought you wasn't gonna take the Lord's name in vain, mister."

"Not in vain, Joey. It's the truth about G-O-D, caps or no caps. Faith ... goddamn faith ... because the big guy—if there is a big guy—doesn't want us knowing certain things. He made that point in the Tower of Babel story—and the Job story. You know them?"

The kid presses his lips together in disgust. "I dunno. But you still can't say them words. It's a sin."

"Well, let's not kick a dead horse, right?"

Joey shrugs.

"You do remember me, right?" Still chewing your lobster roll, you wipe your mouth with the back of your hand and say, "The fiver I gave you to go to Ben and Jerry's?"

He nods. Smirks. "Hot-fudge sundae," he says.

"Well, I got just one question for you, my pal Joey, and it might be worth another hot-fudge sundae for you. That is, if I get the right answer. Sound okay to you?"

The boy nods, as you knew he would.

"So, ... do you remember the dog that was with me last time I was here?"

Joey's eyes dart off to the passenger seat of the Jeep. "Yeah. I guess. Sorta."

"Sorta? Why sorta, kid?"

The kid flinches at the challenge. "Well," he says, glancing first over at you and then back to the Jeep where he fixes his eyes, "I kinda remember a dog, but not that one."

Which is when you slap your forehead, more a gesture than an actual slap. "Of course!"

***

After fifteen minutes or so grilling Joey about the difference between the two dogs, Dumbass and BadBreath, even demanding that the kid confirm that he'd never seen this one—Dumbass—ever before, which he does, you make the boy promise and then promise again:

"Yeah, mister, I promise I ain't never seen that dog before."

"I have never seen," you can't stop yourself from correcting.

"I don't know what you seen, mister, but I never ever seen that black dog in my life." He points at Dumbass.

But even then you aren't done with your questions, now chattering aimlessly about the Red Sox and the damn traffic on the Cape and the rain forecast for the weekend, then deftly slicing in a question certain to confuse the kid about what he remembers—or doesn't remember—about the last time you saw each other. All the while snapping photo after photo of the kid, who patiently—or maybe not so patiently—keeps waiting for the fiver so he can hop on the bike and race up to Ben and Jerry's.

"Mister, for the last time, I ain't seen you since you gave me that five-dollar bill—and I ain't seen this new dog. Though he don't look like no puppy." Then he nods, wide-eyed, no doubt hoping you haven't forgotten all about the bribe. "Did I answer your question okay?"

"You did, kid. Thank you. Really. And I'm sorry, I'm sorry I've been such a … hmmm … pain in the butt—is it okay to say that?"

The boy nods wide-eyed as if he's wondering what is coming next. You reach into your pocket and pull out a thin roll of bills, thumb through the ones until you find a five, and hold it out.

Joey snatches it and quickly jumps back on the bike. He is about to pedal off when you call out, "Hey, wait."

Both hands on the handlebars and standing up over the banana seat, he turns his head and scowls. "What?"

You rip off another five from the wad in your hand, walk over to the bike, and stuff the bill into Joey's back pocket. "This one's for the time you might not remember seeing me—and the mutt. Consider it tomorrow's banana split."

"Hot-fudge sundae."

"Right. Just testing you."

Joey shrugs, places his dirty sneaker on the high pedal, and races off.

Waiting until the boy is out of sight, you slide back into the Jeep, cup Dumbass's block head, then spin your wheels getting back on Route 6. You are, of course (of course!) headed back to Newport and the Sunoco to speak with Manny. And hoping Mr. Cardozo won't spot you—and wondering what you'd do if that sonofabitch does.

You flip the turn signal that hasn't worked in a year or two and brake into the gas station so that you can drive by the bays to see if the kid's old man is around.

The bay doors are open, but you only see the old tattooed and ponytailed mechanic in there working on someone's Audi. So you pull up on the window side of the pumps.

At the pump, you lean over to see if you can spot Manny or Cardozo in the shop. Manny is at his usual place behind the counter, but the afternoon glare makes it impossible to see anything else. So, you mutter, "Well, fuck it, a man's gotta do what a man's gotta do," and pat Dumbass on the rump, telling him to sit up straight—he doesn't—and then wander around the back of the Jeep and over to the glass door.

Manny is frantically waving a finger as you open the door to the shop, pointing insistently toward the bathroom. But you continue to walk in, amble over to the counter.

"Okay, okay, okay," you whisper, "this'll be quick." You reach into your pocket, pluck out the twenty-dollar bill that was just behind the second five you gave Joey. Lay it on the counter and push it over. Manny looks like the blood has all drained from his head. "Gimme twenty on Pump Two," you continue to whisper, "and answer me one question."

Just as Manny nods, still pale, still not breathing, you hear the noisy hand drier in the bathroom. Then moments later the door squeaks open.

You stand stock still waiting to hear it close but hear only footsteps coming your way ... and as you hold your breath, preparing to turn around and hold up your hand in defense or peace, you see Manny's face relax and hear the click of the doorknob as the man goes back into the garage.

"Well, that was really fuckin' close. What d'ya think he'd have done to me?"

Manny is still too rattled to talk, but he picks up the twenty, slides it into the cash register, and punches a few numbers into the machine on the counter. "You should go now," he says under his breath.

"I'm going," you reply, holding up the same hand you would have held up to fend off Raul. "But first I have an easy question for you. Okay?" Manny shakes his head in disbelief. "Okay?" you say a little louder and an edge more gruffly.

Manny presses his lips together and nods.

"Well, I want you to look out that window and let me know if you see man or beast sitting in the passenger seat of my Jeep."

Manny inhales deeply through his nose and holds his breath. Then he turns his head very slowly as if he were afraid of what he might see. "Nothing," he finally whispers toward the window.

You can see Dumbass sitting there like a kid's stuffed animal. "That was too quick. Much too quick. Look again—and really look this time. The passenger seat of my Jeep."

Manny again turns to look in the direction of the Jeep, but now he is trembling. "Please mister," he whispers toward the window, "Please go. I don't see nothing."

"You don't see anything."

"Right. I don't see nothing."

"This is not a test, Manny. I just want to know if you see a person or a statue or a sculpture or maybe a dog on the seat?" Manny now looks like he is in a trance. "A refrigerator, a hot dame, anything at all?"

You bang the counter with the side of your fist. "Manny! I'm done tiptoeing around ... do you see a dog in the passenger seat of my Jeep?"

White-faced, Manny shakes his head, then looks down at the counter cluttered with lighters and rolling papers and small caffeine shots and flinches at the sound of a pneumatic drill in the garage.

"I'm sorry, son. I really am. But now I really got something to ponder."

Manny nods. Holding his breath again.

"Take a breath. I'm going. I am going. And I am sorry I've caused such distress in your life."

And seconds later you are striding out the door, safely out of sight on the other side of the Jeep, filling up your twenty dollars' of regular and pondering what can only be called the imponderable.

***

By the time you get back to Ledge Road, Dumbass lumbering behind as you pointlessly hold the door open and walk into the kitchen. Sarah is cutting up peaches. There is pie crust already pressed into the plate at her side. She looks up with a smile. "Hey, good news," she smiles. Andrew and Cecilia and the kids are coming over for dinner tonight." She points to a couple of thick sirloins on the counter. "Make yourself useful and check to see if we have propane so you can grill them up."

You walk over to the steaks, push a finger in one of them for no good reason, and think, *this is gonna be good.*

"What are you smirking about?"

"Nothing." You smirk. "Nothing."

"Something."

"Oh Christ, Sarah, do you have to know everything?"

"Yes." She goes back to slicing peaches. "This whole family would fall apart if I didn't keep tabs on each of you."

"As if—"

"As if you weren't all children."

"Oh, Christ ... if you must know, I'm just pleased as punch with the idea of chewing some good red meat with my politically correct son and his New Age family."

"You are incorrigible!"

"I am." You cough out a laugh. "If I remember, that was exactly—or as close to exactly as I'm going to get—what you said the first time we met."

Now Sarah is smiling, first curiously then broadly, not turning her head, still cutting up peaches. "True then, true

161

now. Tigers and stripes and all that nonsense, Charlie. Forty, fifty pounds heavier and that horrid smoker's cough notwithstanding, you are the same infuriatingly arrogant"— she glances up quickly before returning to the peaches—"cute boy I met at that silly 'smoker' at Holyoke." She tilts her head and turns again to look at her husband. "Whatever happened to those children we once were, Charlie?"

"Nothing, sweet girl," you say without a hint of irony. You walk over and wrap your arms around her, burying your nose in her hair, inhaling her eternally luscious scent. "We're still here. Always here." And before you can stop yourself, "Always who we were … and as I'm just beginning to understand, always and ever a part of who we're destined to be."

"I don't know about that," she says, tilting her head back onto his shoulder. "But I do know we'll be destined to be very hungry if you don't find out about the damn propane tank." A shake of her shoulders lets you know the hug is over.

And two hours later, the pie in the oven, potatoes boiling on the stove, salad on the counter, you walk back into the house with the propane tank you had picked up at the U-Haul on Connell Highway, holding the screen door an extra second to let the fat old dog scoot in. Again, as if that is necessary.

"More good news," Sarah says. "Dylan's in town and coming over, too. Just like old times."

Then she grows silent, maybe realizing the idea of old times simply isn't true anymore. Hasn't been true for years. Or at least that's what you think the silence is all about. "Yep, them old times, darling," you say, affecting some northeast version of a Texas drawl. "I can mosey on back to practically any time in my life—our life—and smell them roses. And sometimes," you add a step or two later, lugging the propane tank toward the patio door, "I can smell 'em comin' up in the future."

"Don't even go there," Sarah calls from behind. "The boys will have you committed to St. Clare's before you can say Jack Robinson."

Chapter Sixteen (or Three or Two): That Evening

Five minutes before Andrew, Cecilia, Jack, and Diane are to arrive—and they always arrive promptly; Dylan always shows up fifteen minutes late—you position yourself in the frayed wingback chair in the living room, reaching down to find Dumbass at your feet.

At first you can't decide whether to fake taking a nap as they walk into the room or to look like you are so engaged in reading that you don't look up … unless and until one or both of the kids notice the dog.

You opt for reading, concerned that if you close your eyes you won't be able to see whether Dumbass is still around when they walk in. Wallace Stevens's *Harmonium* is on the cherry table next to the chair, right where you had left it after remembering that long-ago exchange with Joni. You pick it up and thumb through until you get to "The Snowman."

Seconds later you hear the kitchen door open and the spontaneous squeals of delight as you imagine Sarah enveloping the two kids in her embrace. Then you hear her say, "Pop's in the living room. Go give him a hug."

You pretend you're reading—pretend to look shocked when the two of them are standing right in front of you, giggles leaking out of their squiggly little mouths, and quickly reach out with both arms and scoop them into your lap. "You almost scared me to death," you say cartoonishly as they howl with delight.

For those seconds you forget about the dog, and when you glance down at the rug, he is gone. But Andrew is standing in the doorway. "Hey, leave them kids alone." He snorts, the smirk on his face betraying his pleasure at the in-joke only he and the old man would understand.

You now wonder whether Dumbass slipped behind the veil when Andrew walked in or ... what? maybe he's just being ornery? In any case, the dog isn't in the living room. And now it doesn't matter, because Andrew, followed by Cecilia, is there, Andrew holding up his hand, saying, "Don't get up," while Cecilia coos, "Don't listen to him ... get the hell up so I can give you a proper hug!"

You ease the kids off your lap and with an unplanned grunt push yourself out of the chair. Cecilia, up on her tiptoes, throws her thin arms around your neck, her head under your chin, and squeezes. "So good to have you back home, Charlie." And when she steps back, you can see her eyes pooling.

You have never figured out why Cecilia likes you so much— even loves you—but then you notice Andrew waiting his turn. "I don't know what I did to deserve you, but I do know what I did to deserve him, though." Then you and Andrew bump chests gingerly and pat each other on the back two times before stepping back again behind the father-son veil.

Which is quickly filled by Sarah's calling out, "Dylan's here!" Which moments later sets off a whole new round of hugs, squealing kids, Sarah yelling from the kitchen to tell you to get the steaks on and ... could it be? ... barking in the backyard.

"Did you hear that?" you say to no one in particular. Andrew, Cecilia, the kids, Dylan, everyone grows quiet.

"What?" Dylan says finally. "My growling stomach? The chimes of freedom? The wind in the willows?"

"No, no, no, barking! Can't you hear it? There's a dog barking. Anyone else hear it?"

"Oh Christ," Dylan says, looking over at Andrew. He whispers out of the side of his mouth but loud enough for everyone to hear, "I think the old coot is hallucinating again."

You're not having it. Not now. You turn and walk out of the living room and into the studio, peer out the windows at the marsh. Dumbass is on the lawn, right in front of the hammock strung up between two pines, barking into the marsh.

"You see BadBreath out there, Dad?" Andrew says, trying to be funny, but there is a tremor in his voice.

"How 'bout St. Augustine?" Dylan adds, no tremor.

You turn to find both sons right behind you. Then glance around them into the living room, where Cecilia and the kids stand, confused smiles on their faces. "Nothing there," you call back. "Must've just been some geese passing overhead."

Diane has her arms wrapped tightly around Cecilia's thigh. Her head is craned back and she looks up wide-eyed at her mother. "Is there a dog? Is there a dog?" she whimpers. "I didn't hear anything." For reasons nobody in the family understands, she has always been desperately afraid of dogs. All dogs. Even BadBreath. Even the little white frufru ones. In fact, them the most.

Then everyone just stands there as if they were playing freeze tag. Except Jack, who sidles up to you and raises his arms to be picked up. And in your hug, he whispers in your ear, "I heard barking."

You glance around at the family still stuck in their places and, breaking the plane, say to everyone but Jack, "Well, Jack"—lowering the boy back down to his feet—"let's go out into the backyard and check out the damnable geese who sound like dogs. And while we're doing that, I'll cook up some of that good red meat that your dad loves so much—and your mean old grammy now only lets me have once a month."

"That's not true!" Sarah calls out from the kitchen, but you know it is true. Then you hold out your hand for Jack, who, smiling triumphantly over at his sister, reaches over and grabs it, each of you thrilled at different things, walking back through the kitchen to pick up the platter of raw steaks.

You can see Dumbass squirming around on his back as soon as you step out the patio door. And when he sees you and Jack, he turns over, sits up, shakes the pine needles off his back, licks his balls, and stands, thick tail wagging.

"Do you see a dog out there?" you say, pointing to the hammock.

Jack squints his eyes and stares out toward the marsh. He nods yes but does not speak.

You lay the platter next to the grill, lift the cover, turned on the gas, and in one motion light a match and toss it on the burners with a whoosh. Dumbass barks again.

"Did you hear that?"

Jack nods. "Yes," he adds in a whisper.

"Why you whispering?" you whisper and shut the hood of the grill.

The boy shrugs. "I don't know. It feels like it's like a secret."

"Huh! Well, maybe it is," you continue to whisper, "but why do you think it's a secret?"

First looking back at the house, then back to you, he says, "I don't think everyone hears the barking. But I do."

"Yeah, me, too." You place your palm over the boy's warm nape. "Tell me this, Jackie; are you sure you see a dog over there?"

"Yup," he says, smiling and, still whispering, adds, "Fat black one. Waggin' his tail."

You contain your relief and joy, and don't say anything for quite a while. Then you sit down in the wrought-iron chair and, reaching around the boy's thin waist, pull him onto your lap. You don't know whether to laugh or cry, so you close your eyes, press your cheek down on the boy's summer crew-cut, and hold him as tightly and gently as you would a puppy. And when Jack begins to wriggle out from the embrace, you whisper, "Do you think that there are any other people who can see the dog?"

Jack doesn't say a word for a while, then shrugs. "I guess so. If I can see it—and you can see it—then somebody else must be able to see it. Just not Diane. She's scared of dogs, you know."

You smile at your grandson's precocious wisdom. "I know. Maybe that's why she couldn't hear the barking. Maybe the rest of them are afraid to see the dog?"

Jack nods his head emphatically several times.

"Do you think that if Diane was out here with us she'd be able to see the dog?"

More silence as you listen to the boy breathing. "I don't know," he says finally. "I kinda think she wouldn't see it. But she wouldn't even open her eyes."

You laugh at the simple wisdom of that statement, a wisdom that is beyond the wise one speaking it. Now you want to explain—to someone, anyone, even an eight-year-old, what you think is really happening, but you know that Jack won't understand—and it would instantly close up the veil the two of you had walked through. Instead, you kiss the top of his head and say, "Well, let's just keep it a secret between the two of us ... at least until someone else in the family sees it. Okay?"

Jack offers another stiff series of nods as you lift him up by the armpits and lower him down to the deck. "Now let's cook these bad boys. You like steak?"

Jack grins. "Yum."

And for no good reason other than to tweak your son, you say, "Your dad ever grill up juicy steaks for you kids?"

Jack grins again. "No! Him and Mommy always say we're not supposed to eat red meat." And when you tousle the boy's head, Jack adds, "Except when we come over here."

"That's right, Jack. When you come over here, it's like stepping into a whole new country." And then you add, "a new dimension of life."

He looks confused.

"You don't know what 'dimension' means?" The boy shakes his head no with a shy smile. "Well," you pause, trying to put it into words an eight-year-old could understand, but quickly realize that would be just another exercise in futility. So, you say, "Would you like to toss the steaks on the grill?"

Jack looks back toward the house to see if anyone is watching. His dad and Uncle Dylan are standing on the patio. Dylan gives him a thumbs-up. "Could I?"

"Absolutely." You hand the long fork over to Jack, pick up the platter, hold it in front of the grill, guide the boy's hand to poke the first cut of meat, pick it up, and transfer it to fire. Then the next. And the next. And when the bloody platter is empty, you and Jack glance back at the patio with big smiles spreading across your faces.

When Dumbass runs off barking, disappearing into the marsh grass, you say out of the side of your mouth, "You hear that?"

"Yup." Jack giggles. Then you hold up your palm so Jack can jump up and give you a high five.

***

Nobody mentions a dog at dinner, not even when the conversation pauses as each of them takes a first bite of the juicy tender steak and buttered baked potatoes on their plates. Not even when Dumbass starts barking again.

You glance down the table at Jack, who tilts his head and laughs out loud, mouth full of meat.

"What's so funny?" Cecilia asks, laughing herself at Jack's infectious laugh.

The boy shrugs. "I don't know. The steak tastes so good, I guess. I just laughed—it's yum! Meat is yum!"

"Oh my God, Dad." Andrew bursts out laughing. "You're going to be the nutritional ruination of my family."

"That's my plan." And then you add, "Seamus Heaney," without any attempt to explain what he or this has got to do with enjoying a good juicy piece of steak:

> "... suddenly you're through, arraigned yet freed,
>   as if you'd passed from behind a waterfall
>   on the black current of a tarmac road
>
> past armor-plated vehicles, out between
>   the posted soldiers flowing and receding
>   like tree shadows into the polished windscreen."

Perhaps if you hadn't spoken similarly uncited and possibly unrelated passages at the dinner table throughout their childhoods, Andrew and Dylan might be worried that you have really lost your marbles—hearing things—seeing things—and are for all intents and purposes one stumbling step away from the nursing home. But as it is, probably nothing seems any different than it always has been, and Dylan picks up his fork (with a piece of steak skewered on the tines) and offers an uncited line from his own world, singing part of a song about a railway station by Brewer and Shipley.

To which Andrew, not to be outdone by his father or his brother, puffs out his chest and recites:

> "'Twas brillig, and the slithy toves
>   Did gyre and gimble in the wabe:
>   All mimsy were the borogoves,
>   And the mome raths outgrabe."

"Thank God you're here, Cecilia," Sarah says. And in the next moment her eyes are pooling. "I'm sorry, everyone. Times like this always make me miss when Joni was around, not only to have her here"—now she forces away the ache with a laugh—"but just to even the odds."

"She's here," you offer before you can stop yourself. "Joni is here."

And in the five second *did he really say that?* delay circulating around the table, you quickly add, patting your chest loudly, "Here, here, here, goddamnit! What's happened? Have you all lost the ability to understand metaphor? Are you all Aspergers?"

"Ass burgers!" Jack howls, Diane giggles, and the adults all laugh, mostly in relief.

And then you are all back in your safe places again. The steak is disappearing bite by bite, only leaving behind blood on the platter, the baked potatoes are gone, the butter is scraped off the bottom of the butter dish, only oily remnants of the salad from Sarah's garden remain in the bowl, the glasses of red wine are empty, and the glasses of water are half sipped.

And when Sarah brings out the vanilla ice cream and warm peach pie, no one is thinking about Joni or St. Augustine or dogs barking. Except you, who think you may have glimpsed Joni standing in the doorway and, reaching down under the table, find Dumbass curled up at your feet.

"So ...," you say and break the plane, "Jack and I were talking out there"—you point out the window to the dark backyard—"about doing a little fishing tomorrow."

You can see Jack look up, mouth slung open, turning toward his dad, who is no doubt wondering what is happening. You know that Jack is as sure that he had seen the dog as he is certain that you two had not talked about fishing, but clearly he doesn't know how to respond to the lie in his name. So, he just stays quiet and watches.

Andrew shifts his eyes toward Cecilia, who shrugs and says, "Why not. He can skip day camp tomorrow."

"So ... it's all right to take him off your hands for a few hours? Leave after breakfast; be home before dinner?"

Jack grins, still wearing that curious look on his face.

"I wanna go fishing, too," Diane says.

Cecilia looks down at the six-year-old—and then glares at Charlie—and waits.

"Oh, you know, sweetheart, I, um, already made arrangements with my friend Mason to go fishing—and he doesn't go anywhere without his dog—" Diane's eyes grow dark with the mention of a dog. "So how about I take you fishing on Saturday?"

She nods but is not convinced that there is not some kind of trick going on there.

Sarah holds her tongue but shoots a scalding glance your way because she knows Mason doesn't have a dog.

And although Cecilia seems satisfied with that solution, Andrew, no doubt wondering what the hell is going on that he is not privy to, says simply, "Sounds good ... I guess now everybody who wants to go fishing with the old coot, gets to go fishing with the old coot. I remember those halcyon days fishing with him."

"Me, too," says Dylan, perhaps a little wistfully.

And that being that, was that.

Until later that night, after the kids and grandkids had left; after you and Sarah, without a word between the two of you, clean up the kitchen and living room, each lost in your own time wars and time warps.

Later still, when you join Sarah in bed with a groan, she turns away from her book. "What are you up to, you devious old man?"

You feign shock, palms up. "What are you talking about?"

Her voice is already rising: "What am I talking about? I'm talking about the fact that Mason doesn't have a dog. What are you up to, Charlie?"

"Nothing." And now your chin recedes into your chest. "Well, no, he doesn't have a dog. That is true." You reach over to the night table to get your book. "But I'd like to spend some private time with Jack."

Not a lie.

Chapter Seventeen (or Four or Three): Next Day

The next morning you are up early, microwaving the dregs of coffee from dinner the night before, slurping it up while standing at the counter next to the refrigerator, grabbing some granola bars out of the pantry and dropping them in your backpack, then scurrying out to the garage to get the rods and the tackle box and tossing bottles of water into the back seat of the Jeep.

When you slide in right next to Dumbass, he yawns, pink tongue curling out of his formerly ferocious mouth. Which somehow leads you to open your mouth in a yawn—and then seemingly out of nowhere, you think about Gene Kelly and somebody else in the movie *Singin' in the Rain* ... but you're pretty sure you've never seen the movie.

"No stranger than some of the things I've experienced the last few months," you say to the dog with a shrug. Then back out of the garage, as usual enamored of that sweet whine of the engine, certain that this is going to be a good day.

First stop: Kingston.

Jack is sitting on the wrought-iron white circular bench around the sycamore tree, fishing rod and small tackle box next to him, when you pull into the driveway. Seconds later Andrew walks out of the classic 1850 saltbox with Diane, too big to be on his hip, on his hip.

Smiling broadly, the two of you gaze at each other on the bluestone path in an ancient kind of generational standoff. "Well, well, well," Andrew begins, "it's old Santiago and Manolin off to get the marlin!"

"Well, truth be told, my famous YA"—air quotes—"writer son, Manolin was forbidden to go in Santiago's boat—and Jack Spratt and I are keeping our feet on dry land, fishing for stripers and bluefish." You follow that with a smile, perhaps a bit too triumphantly.

"I stand corrected, you self-righteous S-O-B," Andrew says with a grin that mirrors your triumphant smirk. "And where, might I ask, are you taking my son fishing for stripers and bluefish?"

"What's a S-O-B?" Diane asks before you have a chance to formulate a snide reply.

You laugh. Andrew laughs. "I am an S-O-B, sweet girl. I am the very definition of an S-O-B. And we are going to go to Sandwich, to the Sandwich marina, to fish off the bulkhead. And then we're gonna go to Gertie's Roadside Rest and get ourselves some sandwiches ... lobster rolls!"

Diane scrunches up her face at the mention of lobster rolls. And from behind you, you hear, "I don't really like lobster." You turn to see Jack looking up at his dad. Now Andrew is beaming. Not fake beaming. Really beaming.

So you take a deep breath and walk through the second or third membrane of the morning. "Not a problem, my Manolin, they have hot dogs, burgers, clam strips, everything you'd ever want."

"I wanna hot dog!" Diane yells and squirms in her father's arms until he lowers her to the lawn. "Can I go, Pop?"

You glance at the Jeep, Dumbass sprawled out on the back bench seat, and don't have the heart to say no. "Hmmm, well, I think I have room in the back seat. Do you think you can fit in the back seat?"

Diane looks at the battered Jeep and nods, eyes sliding back and forth, nodding some more. She has no idea Dumbass is back there. Or was there. Dumbass has disappeared.

So you glance over at your skeptical son and speak directly to him: "Well, sweetheart, if it's all right with your dad …"

Andrew folds his arms across his chest. "I thought Mason—and his d-o-g—were coming along?"

"Backed out—as usual," you mumble quickly. "Can't ever count on that S-O-B to follow through."

"I thought you're the S-O-B, Pop?" Diane giggles.

"I am. I am. I really am. But Mason is a different kind of S-O-B."

Moments later, Jack's rod and tackle box are stowed away in the back of the Jeep, and you, Jack, and Diane are buckled into the old heap, ragtop folded down.

And some forty minutes after that, you leading the kids in endless choruses of "Octie the Octopus" and "There was an old lady who swallowed a fly," two songs their parents had banned from all car rides because of the unrepentant violence in each, you pull up to the Sandwich bulkhead at the Sandwich marina.

You look all around for Dumbass, but the dog is nowhere in sight. Then you leave the kids sitting on a weathered wooden bench to go buy some bloodworms and mackerel at the bait shop.

Dumbass is lying in the corner of the shop. Under a NO DOGS ALLOWED sign. He doesn't acknowledge your presence, either by raising his big head or flopping his tail. You mutter, "So it goes."

So you return to the car a few minutes later with the bait and hook up belly sections of mackerel to each hook on the Sabiki rigs you brought along for the light rods. And three sticky buns, two cans of Sprite, two bags of Skittles, two Styrofoam cups of lukewarm brown water posing as coffee, three trips to the smelly bathroom, and one more bag of mackerel later, the three of you have reeled in two cunners, one perch, and a small sea bass, which to Diane's delight you deem the "Catch of the Day."

None were "keepers," you try to explain using far too many words, but neither of the kids seems upset, instead beaming as you take cell-phone photographs of each one holding a fish—making sure to include in the frame the Skittles and Sprites—and immediately text them off to what you know will be their disapproving parents.

***

Sometime after noon, you pull into the gravel lot at Gertie's Roadside Rest, cut the engine, wait until the dieseling has stopped, and then tell the kids to wait in the Jeep while you check out the menu board.

You slide out and look all around for Dumbass and Joey. After all, they are the unspoken point of this whole adventure, what you used to call "subtext" when teaching your photography students at Salve Regina.

Unfortunately, neither boy nor dog is anywhere to be seen. So you take the kids by the hands to the moldy bathroom around back of the stand, wash their sticky hands as best you can, and then walk them to a picnic table behind the gravel lot. Tell them to wait again while you get a hot dog for Diane, a cheeseburger for Jack, a lobster roll for yourself, three paper baskets of fries, and, really tempting extreme parental disapproval, cups of syrupy soda-machine Coke all around.

The kids can't believe their good luck. Fishing, sticky buns, Sprites, Skittles, hot dog, cheeseburger, and now this, Cokes! They tell you they can't wait to get home and tell Mommy and Daddy about "the greatest day ever!"

You wince. Then smile.

With a mouthful of cheeseburger and fries mashed together in his molars, Jack seems to be staring out at the field behind the parking lot.

"What you see out there, bub?"

Jack squints. "I don't know. Something black way, way, way out there," he whispers and points toward the tree line. "A dog maybe."

Hearing the word "dog," Diane presses herself against you. "I don't want a dog here," she whines.

Seconds later, just as Dumbass has somehow transported himself to the gravel lot, you watch as the old dog slowly and achingly climbs up into the front passenger seat of the Jeep. You you wrap your thick arm around the skinny little girl's shoulder and press her close. You assure her that there are no dogs around. Glance across the table to wink at Jack.

Just then you hear crunching gravel and skidding tires, followed by that familiar girlish voice. "Hey, those your grandkids, mister?"

"Joey!" you exclaim, perhaps too joyfully. Joey, still straddling the bike, backs up a few feet. "Just the man I wanted to see."

Joey's face grows red as he smirks, "I ain't no man, just a kid."

"Well," you say, "I think you're gonna help me answer some man-sized questions in a little bit. But first, yes, these are my two grandkids, Jack and Diane. You know John Cougar Mellencamp?"

Joey looks confused.

"He's a song writer. Wrote a little ditty about Jack and Diane." The boy shrugs and glares at the two kids sitting on either side of Charlie and glaring back at him. "Are they good Christians?"

"You mean, unlike their heathen grandfather? Well, there's a rather complicated adult answer to that question, but I don't think so." Another pause as Joey's confusion races across his face. "However, for present company and this rather odd situation we find ourselves in, I'd just say, 'Why not. In fact, hell yeah! Yee hah!'"

Joey giggles at the "Yee hah!" but his countenance quickly grows dark. "You're not s'posed to say that word either, mister."

Using every bit of restraint you have not to tell the kid to mind his own business, you take a deep breath, step through what you imagine is another thin membrane, and respond in what the grandchildren might think is a most un-Pop-like manner. "Well, Joey, I suppose you're right. I shouldn't have said it. But first, as if you couldn't tell, this one's Jack." You place your palm on top of Jack's head. "And this cutie pie is Diane," moving your hand to Diane's shoulder. "And this," you say, extending your arm across the table, "is my pal Joey." Joey scrunches up his face.

The three kids don't speak. Of course.

"And if you all play your cards right, I'm gonna take all three of you up the road for hot-fudge sundaes." You lean your chin across the table toward Joey. "Work for you?"

Joey nods.

"And what about you two ragamuffins?"

Diane looks wary, a bit scared of what might be coming. Jack looks like he is about to be tricked—a face his dad wore often when he was young. But both nod when you look them in the eyes.

"So, my little guinea pigs—"

Diane giggles. "We're not gimmee pigs, Pop! We're girls and boys. Don't you know that?"

Filled with unfathomable love for this golden child, you say, "I'm learning, Diane. I'm learning. But right now, let me tell you what I want you to do for that hot-fudge sundae." Each one nods.

"This is like the game I spy, but I'm going to be the one to say 'I spy ... something,' and then you are going to tell me whether you spy the same exact thing. Got it?"

179

You lower your chin and look at each child, not moving along until each one nods back. Joey is last to agree.

"But I'm going to have to play this game with each of you, one at a time. So, Jack and Joey, I want you two boys to go over there into the field and wait for me. If you want to play catch, there's a tennis ball in the glove compartment of the Jeep. Got it?"

"Got it," Jack says, in effect positioning himself as the more important player in this little drama.

You watch the two boys wander off to the parking lot in their t-shirts and shorts. They are about the same size, but Joey walks like he knows something Jack might never know—and vice-versa. And as they approach the Jeep, Dumbass maneuvers his way through the front seats and with a small but heavy leap plops down on the back bench.

When they're safely far away, Diane squeaks, "How do you know that boy, Pop?"

You laugh at the squeaky voice. "Oh, Christ, sweet girl, it's a long, long story, but I met him a while back when I came here to eat a lobster roll, and I—" You don't finish the sentence, because you have no idea how to explain any of it to a six-year-old.

It doesn't matter, though. Diane has already moved along: "Let's play I spy, Pop."

You squeeze her in a hug and, in one motion, move her onto your lap. "Yes, let's play I spy. Should I go first or do you want to go first?"

"You, Pop."

"Good. So ... I spy a tall pole made of wood."

"A tree!" she cries, already thrilled with the game. "Now it's my turn. I spy ... something kinda red with feathers."

"Oh, that's a tough one ... ketchup bottle?"

She giggles. "Nooooooo, Pop!"

"A hat?"

"Noooooooo!"

There is a father and son playing with a kite out in the field. Charlie points. "A kite?"

"Nooooooo!" again, but now she is about to burst in her delight at your ignorance, so you figure it's time to make your move. You point over near the building. "Is it a bird?"

"Yes!" she screams as you hug her into your chest.

"Whew! I didn't think I was ever going to figure it out. Now it's my turn."

And so the two of you go back and forth with your silly "I spy"s until you bring her eyes closer and closer to the Jeep. You glance over to the field and see Jack and Joey lazily tossing the tennis ball back and forth, then say, "I spy something black and furry."

Diane is silent for a while, longer than you want, so you repeat, "I spy something black and furry."

"A dog!" she cries, though not exclusively out of fear. You can hear some joy in her voice.

So you pick her up under those skinny arms, turn her around, and plop her bottom down on the picnic table. You want to look her in the eye. "Did you really see a dog?"

"Yup!" She giggles.

"A real dog?"

"Yup!"

"What color?"

"Black."

"Right."

"In your Jeek," she adds.

"Right. And"—you pause—"you're not afraid?"

Now she pauses. Shakes her head. "No."

"How come?"

She shrugs. "Don't know." Another shrug. "I'm just not."

"Would you like to pet him?"

She shakes her head no.

"I'll take you over there and hold you. You can reach over the side of the Jeep and just touch his soft fur. How's that sound?"

She shakes her head again.

"How about if I hold you tight and we just wander over there so you can just look at him from close up?"

Her eyes now moving back and forth between the Jeep and you, Diane finally nods.

"Atta girl," you say, and before she has time to change her mind, you swivel off the bench, lift her onto your hip, and stride over toward the parking lot, her skinny arms tight, then growing tighter, around your neck.

Dumbass is sitting up in the passenger seat as you approach, but of course he doesn't seem particularly interested in visitors, one way or the other.

"You still see him?" you whisper as you approach the hood.

Diane doesn't answer, just squeezes your neck tighter, her smooth cheek against your rough and wrinkled face.

"Ready?"

More nodding. Diane's arms relax from the death grip around your neck as she mirrors the pose of the dog.

But just as you pass the headlight, Dumbass moves over to the driver's seat and then, with surprising grace and dexterity, leaps out of the car and starts trotting back toward the field where the two boys are still playing catch.

"Bye-bye, doggie," she says.

"Yeah, bye-bye is right." You hike her back up on your hip and start to walk off to the boys, but stop to watch Dumbass saunter in between the boys, the tennis ball soaring right over his head then bouncing off to Joey's left.

Now Jack is pointing in Dumbass's direction. Joey picks up the ball and is winding up to throw it back when he sees Jack pointing. He turns his head, nods, and tosses the ball again.

Nothing has happened, but it is clear to you that both boys have seen the dog. Dumbass is now passing by the boy and his dad flying a kite farther out in the field, the kite losing altitude and going into a death spiral, heading right toward the dog.

Dumbass doesn't flinch at the missile heading his way. And neither the boy nor the dad seems to notice the dog as the kite appears to pass right through the thick black-furred body, coming to rest on the grass.

By the time the boy reaches the dormant kite, its long tail rippling slightly in the soft breeze, Dumbass is way back in the field, disappearing behind the tree line.

"Did you see that, darling?" you ask, wondering how that word—darling—had entered your vocabulary.

"See what, Pop?" She drops her arms from around your neck and takes your face between her hands, pressing your lips together in a funny face, giggling through her words. "Chubby baby, chubby baby."

You speak but sound like a cartoon character, which makes Diane giggle more, and she kneads your cheeks like they're dough.

You are about to growl at her to stop, like you used to growl, half jokingly, half deadly serious, at Andrew, Dylan, and Joni when they got too silly. But just then Jack and Joey race over. Diane drops her hands from your face and leans back on your elbow, arms at her sides.

"I won!" Jack yells breathlessly.

Joey shrugs as if to say *I wasn't even trying,* then yanks on Charlie's shirt. "When're we gettin' ice cream, mister?"

"Patience, son. I got some questions for you first." You look first at Jack and then back to Joey. "Did you see the dog that passed between the two of you while you were playing catch?"

"Yup."

"Describe him."

Joey wags his head back and forth. Then lifts his chin. "Black. Fat."

"Good."

"Now can we go?"

"No." You hold up your index finger as if to say *Don't rush me*. Then turn to Jack. "You see the dog?"

Jack smirks like you're sharing some secret. "Yup." Then presses his lips tight together.

"Yeah, and ... " You move your free hand in a big circle.

"Just like that kid—"

"Joey," you say then, in your teacher voice.

Jack looks like he has been reprimanded. "I dunno," he says, instantly subdued. "I guess, just like that kid, Joey, said, fat. Black." And just when you are feeling guilty for grumbling at the boy, Jack adds, "The same dog from last night."

You smile broadly and give the boy a thumbs-up. "Fabulous!" Then after you hike Diane back up on your hip again, you reach over and pull the boy over to your other hip. "You just made this old man ... both of you ... all three of you ... made this old man very happy."

"Now can we have ice cream?"

"Almost." All three groan. You let go of Jack, then slowly lower Diane back down to the grass. Rub your aching elbow. Look back across the field. "I've got another question or two for all of you. Then we can go."

Six bright eyes are now looking up at you. "Okay. Who saw the dog walk between the boy and his dad flying the kite?"

The three kids keep looking at you, now with varying elements of concern written across their faces. No one says a word.

"Any of you?" You point to where the boy and his dad had been flying the kite, but they have gone now.

"Well, what if I didn't?" Joey asks. "Do we still get ice cream?" Jack nods. Diane nods.

You glance back at the empty Jeep. Then out to the empty field. No dog. No boy or his dad. No kite.

But you'd gotten what you'd come for. And more. "Who wants ice cream?" you hear yourself say.

The three kids, being kids, scream in unison, "I do!"

And you recite the old ditty with tears clouding your eyes, "I scream, you scream, we all scream for ice cream."

Chapter Eighteen (or Five or Four): Later and Later Still

Diane is sitting on her mom's lap and chattering away about the fishies she caught and the Skittles and the sticky buns and the Coca-Cola and the hot dog and the boy named Joey and the hot-fudge sundae ... and then, placing her hands on either side of her mom's face so she can't look away, she says, "And I saw a dog and"—squealing now—"and I didn't even cry!"

Cecilia looks back at you, a smile that is more a scowl. "It's true," you say. "We had some kind of canine breakthrough."

"What happened?" she asks coolly.

You shrug.

"I mean, what do you think happened?"

Unable to hide your glee: "I don't know. Maybe it was the Skittles. Or the Coke."

Cecilia helps Diane off her lap, then says to her kids, "Why don't you two go outside and play. I want to talk to your grandfather about some other things. Grown-up things."

And when the kids are gone, Cecilia turns to you. "Charlie, you old coot ... what were you thinking sugaring up my kids and feeding them crap like that?" She is still scowling, but the scowl is rimmed by a smile, so you figure that she isn't really all that mad. But then the smile fades away. She lays her hand on your wrist. "And what's with that boy the kids were talking about?"

"Oh, that kid," you say, scrambling around, buying time, behind what you hope looks like an affable scowl. "He's just a funny kid I ran into a while ago when I stopped in Sandwich for a lobster roll. Took some interesting photographs of him.

And, by the way, it's the best roll on the Cape," you add, hoping that will be the end of that phase of her inquiry.

"No, I meant, what was he doing there?"

"Oh, I don't know. His mom works at Gertie's—and he must've just ridden his bike over there. Nothing I planned. Just a kid who played catch with Jack while Diane and I played I spy."

Cecilia takes her hand from your wrist and, sitting up, puts her arm around your thick shoulders. "I don't know, old man, I don't like this. Feels to me like you got something up your sleeve."

You hold your bare arms straight out. "Not a thing, my dear. What you see is what you get."

"You know, Charlie, I don't come with all the 'grumpy dad baggage' my dear husband drags around with him, but I have to say that this feels awful fishy." She makes some quick air quotes and then adds, "That's not a pun, Charlie. What's up?"

You turn your hands over to show her your palms. "There is nothing going on, Cecilia. Really. We went fishing, caught some fish, ate a lot of junk food, and Diane saw a dog and didn't melt down."

You turn your head and look at her. For a second—through shifting peripheral vision—you realize how much she looks like Joni, and you still your quivering chin by pressing your lips together. "Okay," you say, nodding now, "let me have it, Ms. Social Worker."

"Well, Charlie, I didn't grow up in that house, so I don't buy into the pain-in-the-ass mythologies your sons have concocted around you, especially in all the years since Joni died." She looks at you and waits until you nod. "And I certainly don't feel a need to placate you like your good wife seems to see as her late-in-life cross."

"Oooh, that's cold."

"Nah, warm."

"And that's why I love you. But—" You stop yourself before you say something you'd regret.

"I love you, too, Charlie, but, all those gruff-Charlie stories aside, I know something is going on. You don't fool me."

Your laugh is hollow. "Yeah. Nothing doing. Nothing going on. And don't think that I haven't heard your husband and Dylan—and yes, even that fool Mason—refer to her as 'the long-suffering Sarah.'"

"Right." She leans over and kisses your scratchy cheek. "And right about poor Sarah. But this is getting me nowhere. So now tell me about that damn dog."

***

"So, tell me about the dog, Ray," Sarah echoes later that afternoon, ostensibly out of that nowhere that keeps popping up.

"What dog?"

Sarah frowns and puts her glass of wine down on the wrought-iron table, the marsh noisy and still behind her. "I got calls this afternoon from your two sons and your beloved daughter-in-law, telling me that you're acting weird and that you're seeing things again." She scrunches up her lips and nods your way, so she won't have to say the words.

"What things?"

"Things that are not there. Like that dog business from last night. And apparently this afternoon with the kids. They're really worried. I'm worried. I don't know what to think."

You close your eyes, and seconds later when you open your eyes you reach across the small table to lay your palm on the back of Sarah's hand. "There's nothing to be worried about, honey. Darling. I'm not hallucinating. I'm not seeing things that are not there. The dog my dear social worker of a daughter-in-law is worried about was just some old mutt we saw while playing I spy with the kids over in Sandwich. And the only reason I mentioned it to Cecilia was that little Diane had some sort of breakthrough and didn't freak out when she saw it."

Sarah nods. Licks her lips. "Okay," she says, "but maybe we should make an appointment with a neurologist anyway, you know, just to make sure." You can't stop the scowl from appearing on your face. "I mean, you did see St. Augustine … and Joni … and some dog when you woke up from that coma."

"It was a goddamn coma!" you erupt, all plaintiveness gone. "What the hell don't you—and those goddamn sons of mine— understand about the vast difference between coma and consciousness?"

As her eyes begin to flood, Sarah looks at you like she is trapped in that nether world between pity and anger, two reflexive emotions of hers that you know well from your forty-something years together. Trapped and speechless in your sometimes-thundering presence.

"I'm sorry I yelled," you say preemptively in the chastised voice that you have recently acquired. "I'm just frustrated. You have to trust me, sweetheart, I am not seeing anything that is not there. Promise." Hand up in the air.

And before she can respond, you're spouting the Wallace Stevens poem that end:

> Which is the sound of the land
> Full of the same wind
> That is blowing in the same bare place
>
> For the listener, who listens in the snow,
> And, nothing himself, beholds
> Nothing that is not there and the nothing that is.

Sarah nods. "Impressive, Charlie, even though I have no idea what you're talking about."

And when you stand and walk around behind her, enveloping her in your arms, she leans her head back on your shoulder.

The two of you stay that way long after you expect her to shrug or relax and let you know it is time to break it off. But she just sits there with her head back on your shoulder. "Y'know," she finally says, all cottony, "I'm too tired to cook. Let's go out."

It's enough to make you cry. And on your way through the kitchen, as you reach for the Jeep keys on the counter, Sarah puts her hand on top of yours. "Ray ... I don't want to get there with my hair looking like a nest—and smelling like cigarette exhaust."

"What the hell does that mean?"

"It means that we'll be driving in my Subaru and will arrive at the restaurant neat and clean and unsmelly."

***

The last person you expect to see at the Smoke House over on Scott's Wharf is Mason. Mason had sworn off red meat during the "Mad Cow" era—and had subsequently turned his anxiety into a crusade against "cancer-inducing, artery-clogging animal fat."

But there he is, smiling and motioning you two over to his table, where he sits with an attractive woman who appears not quite young enough to be his daughter, but certainly old enough to know better than to be buying Mason's charming brand of bullshit.

The closer you come to the table, though, weaving your way toward the back of the patio, the closer his date comes to approximating Mason's age. She is wearing a white halter top, which you consider a bad fashion choice for a sixty-something-year-old woman.

You speak first, cutting off Mason as he is extending his hand to introduce Christina. "I thought you didn't eat this kind of hormone- and antibiotic-riddled poison ...." You're already grinning at your own wit.

"Didn't I tell you?" Mason says to Christina. "This is the guy. This is the one I was just telling you about." He laughs, maybe a bit ruefully. "Almost makes me believe in harmonic convergence. Anyway," he quickly adds, extending his hand, gesturing first to the woman, "Christina Hazard, I'd like you to meet"—he shifts his hand—"my old-as-dirt college roommate Charlie Messina and his long, long, long, oh-so-long-suffering wife, Sarah Bascomb."

Sarah had to have known that you wouldn't want to sit with Mason or Christina Hazard, but she accepts their invitation quickly before you have a chance to concoct an excuse. And then, after Mason offers a brief bio of his newly hatched relationship with Christina, whom he had met at a Methodist church excursion up the Connecticut River to the Gillette Castle, all you can find to say is, "Eating red meat, going to church, going on organized excursions ... I mean, what the hell is going on? I don't recognize you. Aliens come and take over your brain?" (You resist the almost all-consuming urge to add, *And, lo and behold, dating an age-appropriate woman.*)

Mason points a thumb over to you and speaks to Christina. "Didn't I tell you?"

"Well," she says, "it's kind of refreshing, isn't it?"

That's when Sarah laughs. "After forty-six years, refreshing might not be the right word." Upon which Mason slides farther into the booth and pats his palm on the seat. Sarah slides into the booth right next to Mason.

And as if to prove her point, you continue to press Mason on his change of diet and his sudden discovery of religion. "I mean, what happened? You get hit by lightning?"

"Although it's possible that the exception proves the rule, people do change, Charles."

"Don't call me Charles," you say, surprising even yourself. A memory wafts in then of the two of you being at the Five Spot on St. Mark's Place ... Charlie Mingus being announced ... Mingus walking up to the mic and saying, "Charlie is a horse's name. My name is Charles" ... and then turning and walking off.

A moment later you are back in the restaurant. "Besides, I don't know what the hell that means, the exception proves the rule."

Mason smirks, probably thinking he is winning. "Think of yourself as the crude exception—and maybe it will all come clear. In the meantime, please sit"—he extends his hand across the table where Christina has already made a place for you—"before I have to go to the chiropractor from looking up your remarkably large and unattractive nostrils any longer."

Having been to this particular rodeo many, many times over the past four decades, Sarah breaks into what she could predict would be increasingly funny then contentious conversation, turning to ask Christina where she lives, what kind of work she does, where she grew up, whether she has family in the area ... that is, more than enough questions to knock both you aging bronco riders off your ridiculous horses ... and the four of you eventually share a rather pleasant dinner. Like regular people.

Or almost like regular people.

Food is good. Conversation good, fun, snarky, easy. And by the time you split the check (two Visa cards in the black folder), the four of you even agree to do it again—soon—though no one actually sets up a date.

And then you grouse all the way home about Mason having no principles. "I mean, the man has no standards, nothing that he stands firm on. He moves through time and space as it suits his convenience ... as if there is no such thing as science or truth."

Sarah listens or seems to listen—staring straight ahead through the windshield and occasionally nodding her head—and then apparently stops listening, opening the glove box and grabbing a classical CD, slipping it into the slot as you continue your decades-old rant about Mason ... until the speakers fill the car with the sounds of Chopin's "Prelude."

Which is when you stop talking.

At least until you realize what she is doing. "Done talking about that spineless friend of mine?"

"I was done a long time ago."

"I mean the man floats through life as if there is no point—" You don't finish, because you were about to tell her about Mason's unrequited love in Key West ... but then realize that as far as she's concerned, Key West never happened.

After blocks of silence, gripping the wheel too tightly, you make a left onto Ledge Road and pull into the garage next to the Jeep. Breathe in. Breathe out. Turn the key. By which time Sarah is already walking over to the kitchen door without waiting for you to catch up to her.

You find her sitting in the living room.

"I know what you're doing," you say.

She closes her eyes. "If only you knew, old man ... I'm just tired of talking about Mason. Yesterday's news."

"Well, I'm not talking about Mason. I'm talking about you insinuating that I was seeing Joni—"

She opens her eyes and leans back into the couch. "And St. Augustine and that dog. Mostly that dog."

"Listen ... forget about the dog and St. Augustine—and Joni, for that matter. They were just portals through which I have simply come to see time. I'm perfectly willing to concede that they were figments"—you shake your head—"nah, products of the coma I was in. But that has nothing to do with the revelation I had after seeing them."

"Yeah?" Now she sounds more curious than worried. "Go on."

"Well, it's not linear, time, like we—like I—always thought. It's overlapping. It's parallel. Everything that has happened is going on in the same moment. Some of which we remember and call a déjà vu—and some which we don't, which we say never happened." You smile, a naked smile. "I'm not sure about the future, though."

"So?"

"So…" Now you're scrambling, Sarah's unexpected "So?" knocking you off-kilter. "So, you are every moment you are alive, getting born, going to first grade, high school, making out with that dipshit from Mineola—"

"Charlie! Get a grip, that was nearly fifty years ago. What the hell?"

But you aren't listening. You're on a roll: "Going to college, getting swept off your feet by that dashing football player, Andrew … Dylan"—you lower your voice—"Joni, everything, all at once."

"What do you think you are telling me?"

You sit there, jaw slung open, waiting for more of the right words to fall from your mouth. You want a cigarette, but know that if you leave the house, the opportunity to speak your truth will be gone. "Well, mostly I'm telling you … that I'm not crazy." You let that sink in for a moment. "And that I'm not ready—yet—to be warehoused with all the senile dribblers and droolers."

"That's not what I'm talking about."

"Yes, you are. And so are my goddamn sons. You all think that I lost it—lost brain cells from that mini stroke or whatever it was—and am one step out of St. Alzheimer's or whatever the place is named."

She presses her lips together and wipes the emerging tears flooding her eyes. "You are a jackass, Charlie Messina. And, as always, you're only half a jackass right."

You tilt your head and feel warm with love, feel yourself passing through some thin membrane. "Better than all wrong, right?" She shakes her head again. "Tell me—"

"Well, I'm worried—and I'm worried for damn good reasons, Charlie. I'm worried about you ... we're old, you passed out, you're seeing ghosts or whatever, you've concocted a whole series of events that never happened."

You are wordless, waiting for another opening to slide in, but she is still forming words of her own. "But to tell you the truth, I am actually also really interested in what you think is happening."

"I just told you what I think is happening—and I think I'm on to something revolutionary."

She gasps. The spell broken. "Oh my God, you really are an arrogant S-O-B."

You look at her like she is a stranger, an intruder. "You never called me an S-O-B before."

Deep breath. In through her nose. Out through her nose. "Not out loud," she says finally. "You've always been a pain in my ass, but it's never been so clear as it is today. You can't possibly think that you're the only one who thinks about whatever you call it, parallel time? It's nothing new."

You sit there unmoving, perhaps a little dumbfounded. "You mean, you think—"

"Yes, my love, you are not the only person on the face of the earth who thinks that this is not all there is." She pats her arm as if to demonstrate the impermanence of flesh. "I'm not going to go down the list, but, you know, I also went to college, and it wasn't simply to marry an arrogant jackass like you. I also studied philosophy and history and literature. It's a long line, Charlie, a long line of folks who have been thinking about the same thing ... and gotten nowhere."

PART V

"I sit with Shakespeare and he winces not. Across the color-line I move arm in arm with Balzac and Dumas, where smiling men and welcoming women glide in gilded halls ... and they come all graciously with no scorn nor condescension. So, wed with Truth, I dwell above the Veil."

— W.E.B. Du Bois, *The Souls of Black Folk*

Chapter Nineteen (or One): Still Later

There I was on the couch that evening, still thinking about Sarah and that long list of thinkers and time travelers, when I drifted off, TV buzzing, into some frustrating dream of trying to load film into a camera and get a picture of Joni. Which was the first thing I thought about when I woke the next morning, sunlight coming in through the east windows making me sweat under the blanket Sarah must have thrown over me when she went to bed.

Maybe I should've been depressed by the eye-opening information Sarah had shared, but, mostly, I felt comforted that I was not alone.

"Also, just for the record," I said aloud to no one, "I wasn't talking about time travel or any of that sci-fi bullshit. I read *Time and Again*, a good beach read, but that's not what I'm talking about—"

"So what are you talking to yourself about?" came a muffled voice from somewhere in the kitchen—not Sarah, not Cecilia, maybe Cecilia?—startling me, my feet, tangled in the blanket, swinging off the couch and onto the rug.

"What the hell?" was all I could come up with.

"It's me, Dad."

"Where? Are you here? Does your mother know? Where are you?"

"Here, there, everywhere. And no, although I sometimes think she understands ..."

I sat there, elbows on my knees, unable to get up. "Am I dreaming? Am I asleep? Am I dead?"

"I don't know. Are you?"

I stared at the empty doorway into the kitchen. "I don't think so." Then I was quiet for a while, trying to sort things out when I grew cold. "Are you still there?" I blubbered out. "I don't think I could handle it if you disappeared again."

"Yes, I'm still here. I'm always here."

"Then where the hell are you?" It was just like old times. An endless déjà vu loop. "Come in here now! I need to see you."

"Oh Christ, this is already getting tedious." That was always her go-to line. She must have said that a thousand times before she died. "I'm not coming in there. And for the record, as I've said countless times, you are not the boss of me, old man."

"You used to say that a lot."

"I had to say it a lot. You're not the easiest father in the world for a girl who wants to try to live her own life."

"So I've been told."

I tried to get up, but my muscles failed me, some great weakness condemning me to the couch. "At least come to the doorway. Let me see you're here."

"I'm here. You don't need to see me."

"Where?"

"Now we're way past tedious." I stared at the empty doorway. "One more time, Charlie: like I said, here, there, and everywhere."

"Don't call me Charlie."

"Noted. You won't make this easy, will you?"

I still couldn't raise myself off the couch. "I'm lost, Joni. At least tell me what you are doing here. Why are you here now?"

"I'm just here. I'm never not here."

"Then, show me something."

"I got nothing to show you. I'm just here. I'm never not here is what I'm telling you."

I managed to straighten up. That made me dizzy. Or what she'd said made me dizzy. Either way, I was so woozy I closed my eyes against the vertigo, but I flinched what seemed like a few seconds later at a smooth wet tongue licking and licking my face.

I swatted it away. Opened my eyes, expecting to see Dumbass, of course, but there was no dog in my face. I glanced around the room and then toward the kitchen. Sarah was standing in the doorway. The dizziness was gone. What might have been a dog disappeared behind her. "Good morning, my dear overweight cross to bear. Did you sleep okay? A little stiff?"

I shook my head and, squinting, tried to look past her.

Sarah must've noticed my confusion. "I couldn't figure out whether to wake you and make you go to bed—and risk having you up all night, tossing and turning and keeping me up—or just let you sleep on the couch and wake up all stiff and sore ... and grumpy."

"Hmmmm."

"Gotta look out for myself sometimes, Charlie. But I took your boat shoes off, in case you didn't know." She pointed under the coffee table.

The phone rang. Sarah turned and disappeared. I heard her voice but couldn't make out what she was saying. I was about to finally push myself up off the couch when she reappeared. "That was someone named Manny; I didn't get his last name—sounded young. He says you left something at the gas station and you should give him a call." She extended her hand with a Post-it pressed between her fingers. "Here's his number."

***

A cup of coffee and a stale bagel and cream cheese later, I was still trying to reconstruct what could only have been a dream about Joni. Or maybe not. I reached across the Jeep to pat

Dumbass's boxy skull and then checked the glove box for the Luckies. Half a pack.

It was Saturday, so the garage bays were closed at the Sunoco when I pulled up to the pumps. The mechanic and Raul were nowhere to be seen, at least from the driver's seat.

I didn't need gas, so I wheeled around and drove over next to the curb by the convenience store window. Manny was inside, taking care of a customer. A female. Long straight hair, her back half-turned to the window so I couldn't see her face. Manny was smiling. Laughing even. I had never seen him happy before.

I decided to wait and let the boy flirt some more, but moments later I lost my patience and swiveled out of the Jeep, strode around the bald spare tire, and yanked open the glass door to the shop. After a quick sweep of the premises ... garage door shut; no one milling around the chip displays; no one at the refrigeration cases. In fact, no one anywhere, just Manny and a giggly teenage girl with brown hair, long enough to cover the waistband of her pink shorts, PINK written across the butt. I shook my head privately at my own time warp, fascinated and appalled all at once.

Manny had looked up when I entered the shop and gave me a nod, as if to say *Don't ruin this for me, all right?* Which I was content enough to do, although I was growing increasingly curious about the "new" Manny I was observing ... talking! animated! laughing! eyes trained on the girl, not the door to the bays, not on me.

I concluded that Manny's old man was not there. Could not possibly be there.

The two kids were talking about how weird it was that Mr. Sherman, their science teacher, I eventually sussed out, was working at Target—in the jewelry department—during the summer. "I know," Manny said, "it's so weird that he has to wait on us ... and be nice about it."

She laughed, of course, and after the lull, which was quickly filled in by the girl—something unrelated to Mr. Sherman, something about her girlfriend going to some "smelly dude ranch out west"—it became apparent that the flirtation was not going to end any time soon. I took a Snapple out of the cooler, ripped a bag of Doritos off the chip rack meandered over to the counter, and pushed them Manny's way.

Manny looked at me and then, as if on cue, the two of us turned to the girl. She was cocoa-skinned—maybe Indian? Pakistani?—and beautiful in the way that children alone can be beautiful, but she was definitely younger than I assumed she would be. I peered out the window and saw there were no cars at the gas pumps—so maybe she wasn't even sixteen.

When it became clear that Manny was having trouble finding the words, I said, "I could use a pack of Luckies to go along with my healthy breakfast here."

I expected the two of them to laugh at my joke, but the girl just lowered her eyes as if she were embarrassed—and Manny found his voice among the ruins of the moment: "Sorry, Alisha, I gotta take—" He didn't finish, because Alisha said in a pubescent-panic-for-no-good-reason that she had to get home and, "maybe I'll see you later?"

"Very nice, Manny," I teased as the glass door slowly closed without a sound.

Manny didn't answer, his gaze on the girl waiting at the crosswalk, then walking across the road, disappearing into the warm air down Maple Street. I slid a twenty onto the counter, looked back at the garage door, and said, "So ... what's this all about?"

Manny pressed his lips together and shook his head. "Nothing. Really." He reached up to the rack above the counter and plucked out a pack of Luckies.

"No, no, no ... not your love life. Frankly, I'm done nosing around in your life. I got bigger fish to fry, lad. I'm here now only to find out why you called me, assuming that I'm the last person in the world you would want to see."

"My dad isn't here."

"Figured." I stared at the boy, who was back in deer-in-the-headlights mode. "So?"

Manny picked up the twenty, punched in the chips, the Snapple, and the pack of Luckies, and, eyes now down on the counter, said, "I saw the dog yesterday. I just wanted you to go—"

"You saw the dog?" I yelped and glanced around to make sure no one had walked in. "You saw it?"

Now Manny was looking out the window. Nodding first, then pointing out toward the Jeep. "Same dog as that one."

I twisted around and saw Dumbass sitting up on the passenger seat. "That dog?"

He nodded.

"Describe it."

After Manny accurately described the old, fat mutt, I asked in the softest voice I could muster, "Is that what you wanted to tell me?"

Manny nodded again, his shoulders finally relaxing down to their natural positions.

"I'm confused," I said, trying to restrain myself. "Why tell me at all? I'm serious. I've brought you nothing but trouble, so why open this can of worms?"

Manny looked confused.

"Is your entire generation incapable of thinking in metaphors? Well, anyway, what were you thinking when you invited me back here?"

A deep breath in and out. "You're gonna think I'm crazy, but I had a dream last night and some girl—maybe older than a girl—came in the shop and told me I had to tell you that I saw the dog."

I held my breath, waiting for the implications of that statement to sink in. "Not so crazy, son. Truth is, I've had a coupla-three weird moments myself the last few nights. Now, tell me what she looked like."

"Hard to say," the boy said. "It was a dream."

"Right. Well then, what color hair did she have?"

He shrugged.

"Long? Short? Straight? Curly? Black? Brown?"

"I dunno, mister. It was a dream."

I reached into my back pocket and pulled out my thick wallet. Fingering past the bills and through the cards and slips of paper, I slid out a photograph of Joni. "This her?"

Manny bent his head forward and looked intently at the photo. "No," he said and shook his head. "I don't think so."

"No, or I don't think so? Don't toy with me, Manny. This is really important."

He seemed to be holding his breath.

"Breathe, son!"

Manny shook his head again. "No. That's not her."

"No? Well, how do you know if you can't even describe what the hell she looked like?"

Another shrug. "I don't know, mister, I just know it wasn't her." His eyes were pooling now.

I felt myself stepping through another membrane. And another. "Okay," I said, all that energy draining out of me. "I'm sorry, kid. I'm sorry. My new mantra. I didn't mean to yell—and I'm very grateful you called and let me know about the dog. That means a lot. More than you'll ever know."

Manny seemed relieved; he was counting out the change when his face went flat as he froze mid-gesture. I spun around to see Raul Cardozo walking into the shop.

We glared at each other, both trapped in the breathless moments between thought and action.

Raul finally broke the standoff: "I thought I told you to stay the hell out of my gas station."

It was not a question. Déjà vu was not quite the right expression for the type of experience I had been living through recently—and I had to quickly swallow the bile that I could already taste in the back of my throat, the same bile that had once driven me headlong into an opposing lineman ... that made me light into the smug faces of generations of jabbering students in my studio classes ... and more than a few times since then into the fat guts of lousy drunks in one or another of Newport's seedier bars.

"You did," I finally muttered and pressed my lips together before the bile erupted into action. "You did." Glancing back then at Manny, I said, "Your son was good enough to give me a call and let me know that I must've dropped my wallet here last time I came in for gas." I held it up, adding, "He's a good kid, your boy."

Raul didn't nod, didn't smile, didn't thank me for the compliment. "You got your wallet, now get the fuck out of my building." He stood there, hands at his sides, blocking the doorway.

I turned and thanked Manny. Then I lifted my chin and turned around, my eyes trained on the powerful man, completely out of character in shorts and a golf shirt, standing in the doorway. Now, with the bile still rising in my throat, I took one step, then another, my eyes growing wide, and said, "If you'll excuse me, sir, I'll take my leave."

Without changing his expression, Raul Cardozo took a half step to the side, creating just enough space to squeeze by, and our shoulders brushed as I pushed open the glass door and stepped out into the already steaming day. I stood there, right on the other side of the door, waiting for the bitter taste to wash away. Then watched an ambulance, lights and sirens going, race down the street.

I was just about to step off the curb and return to the Jeep when I heard Raul berating the boy: "What the fuck was that all about? Hah? I told you to never fuckin' allow that piece of shit back in this station."

"But—" Manny began.

"No buts!" he yelled. "You do as I fuckin' say or you're going to be one sorry little jackass!"

Then there was silence, just the disappearing whine of the siren and some road traffic. I stood there, back to the door, staring out into traffic and urging myself to move along. I took a step off the curb when I heard the door open behind me and felt Cardozo's hot breath on my neck, hands slamming my shoulder blades, sending me stumbling and tumbling to the ground, breaking my fall with my palms and rolling over onto my back.

"Don't hurt him, Dad! Please. He just came to get his wallet and—"

"And what? you little ingrate ... what?" I looked around to see the father pushing the boy back inside the shop, door closing slowly behind them.

Something crashed in the shop, and I heard Manny scream, "No, no! I'm sorry, Dad, I'll never—no! please ..."

Which was about all I could take. I scrambled up off the pavement like I was thirty years younger and barged back into the shop just in time to see Raul behind the counter, fist in the air, and Manny nowhere to be seen. "You hit that kid," I yelled, "and I'll have the cops throw your cowardly ass in jail."

Cardozo stood there stunned, apparently confused to see me back in the store. Seconds later, though, he was storming out from behind the counter, knocking displays over, and, like some fuming bull, thick hands like horns pushing me back against the door, the door swinging open behind me, I tumbled backward onto and then off the curb and onto the pavement as the dog leaped from the passenger seat and lunged at the white-faced attacker, knocking him to the ground, standing over him and barking viciously.

In the ensuing chaos, me sitting dazed on the pavement, Dumbass barking and barking at Cardozo lying on the curb, not allowing the man to get up, Manny reappeared behind the glass door. I struggled to get up, intent on pulling the dog off the man, but Dumbass disappeared as quickly as he had shown up, leaving Raul Cardozo flat on his back, hands clutching his chest, eyes wide open, devoid of anything but fear.

I glanced back toward the Jeep to see if the dog was there. He wasn't. And then down at Cardozo, then up, yelling at the stone-faced boy behind the glass: "Manny! Call 9-1-1!"

**

A half hour later, the paramedic putting away the paddles glanced up and asked Manny what hospital he wanted his dad transported to, "Sacred Heart or Newport?"

Manny looked confused.

"Whichever one's closer," I told the EMT.

He nodded and raced out of the convenience store and over to the rig, lights flashing, to join his partners still bent over the patient, a tube down the man's throat, IV in his arm, eyes closed. A moment later the back doors were shut, sirens screaming as the ambulance pulled out of the gas station toward Newport Hospital.

An out-of-body sensation came over me, making me feel like I was hovering over the scene, jaw hanging open, when I realized that I had my arm around Manny.

I gripped his thin shoulders as I would my own grandson's, but I was unable to find the words that would assure the boy that his father was not going to die. I couldn't speak. Couldn't step through the membrane, thin as it seemed.

Perhaps it was because I was sure the man was already dead. And to lie seemed worse than getting stuck behind another veil.

I know it sounds ridiculous, but in that moment, which was speeding by like an ambulance, I recalled Conrad's lines from *Heart of Darkness*: "There is a taint of death, a flavour of mortality in lies - which is exactly what I hate and detest in the world - what I want to forget. It makes me miserable and sick, like biting something rotten would do."

Then seemingly out of that same nowhere, there was a policeman standing in front of us, notepad in one hand, looking at the mess inside the convenience store, the tear-stained face of the boy, the scrapes and bruises all over my bare arms and legs. He glared at me. "What the hell happened here?"

Manny was apparently incapable of speech. Not me, though. I had something to say. I was going to say it. But when I parted my lips, I understood that while there was a story to tell—a true story—it was not the only story that had led to Raul Cardozo lying lifeless on the pavement. "Well, the short version is that I had had a"—air quotes—"run-in with Mr. Cardozo some time ago and he banished me from his gas station." The cop nodded, scribbled some notes on his pad and looked up again.

"Go on ..."

"But I had to go back to the gas station to"—I glanced over at Manny, squeezed his shoulder—"pick up my wallet. I had left it behind the last time I got gas."

"Yeah, so?"

"Well, Mr. Cardozo became angry when he saw me—understandably furious, I might add—and he pushed me out the door." I held out my scraped arms, lifted my bleeding leg as evidence. "And while he was screaming bloody murder at me to leave, he had what looked like a heart attack, clutching his chest and falling to the ground."

The cop looked at me, then Manny. "That's it?" I nodded. Manny just stared out into the distance.

"Son?"

Manny seemed to nod. Hard to say where he was at that moment. "And you," the policeman said and turned back to me. "You never hit him?"

"Oh no ... I mean, Christ, maybe I shouldn't have shown up while he was there, but it's Saturday and I thought it was safe to come by. But no"—I shook my head—"I never hit the man. Never once. He pushed me out the door and I fell down." I showed the cop my bruises again.

He turned to Manny. "Is that true, son?"

Still staring into the nothingness of gas pumps and traffic, Manny nodded.

And the cop nodded back, but before flipping the notepad closed and sliding the pen into his breast pocket, he glared at me once more. "I'll need your name, phone number, address. You live around here?"

I didn't answer, just reached into my back pocket and pulled out my wallet. I handed him my license and stood, chest rhythmically rising and falling, until the officer finished writing and, extending the license my way, said, "Don't leave town."

"I'm not going anywhere."

And when the officer turned and began walking back to his cruiser, I called out, "I am going to take the boy to the hospital."

The cop didn't seem to hear, sliding into the passenger seat of the cruiser, lights still flashing.

I reached around and squeezed Manny into my side again. "I'm gonna take you over to the hospital, son. But maybe you should call your mom first—and lock up the shop."

Manny nodded, but it seemed that he was still unable to speak. The same vacant look in his eyes. Released from my grip, still staring into whatever abyss lay out in front of him. He reached into his back pocket and plucked out his phone, punched in a few digits and brought it to his ear. A few seconds later I could hear a muffled voice at the other end, but Manny still wasn't speaking.

"Let me," I said, reaching over for the phone. "Mrs. Cardozo?"

"Who is this?" came a heavily accented voice. *"Onde é Manny?"*

"I'm sorry," I said, "I didn't quite get that."

"Where is Manny?" she said, her voice at the high-pitched edge of hysteria.

"Manny is right here, ma'am. He's fine. I am Charlie Messina, I live nearby the gas station in Newport—and was here when your husband ... uh, fell." I glanced at Manny. "I think he might have had a heart attack—and the paramedics are taking him to the hospital. Newport Hospital."

I waited through the silence at the other end. "Are you still there, Mrs. Cardozo?"

"Who is this?" came another voice, a younger voice, an angry voice, a woman with no accent.

I repeated myself and explained again what had happened, skipping over all the shoving and screaming that had gone on before Raul collapsed—and the barking that had gone on afterward. "I'll take Manny over to the hospital—Newport Hospital on Friendship Lane—and I'll wait with him until you show up."

After poking at the Off button and handing the phone back to the boy, I said, "Give me the keys. I'll lock up. The we'll go over to the hospital and wait for your mother. You wait for me in the Jeep."

Manny did what he was told, still looking like he was wandering through a wind storm. I watched him open the half door and slide into the passenger seat. Dumbass was gone.

It took me a while to find the electric panel to shut off the lights and the pumps—they were on the wall next to the filthy bathroom. Then, after resisting the temptation to grab some beef jerky off one of the displays, I locked the glass door and paused on the narrow sidewalk. Looked all around. Manny sat stock still in the Jeep. Still no dog anywhere.

Chapter Twenty (or you know ...): Later

On the drive to the hospital, I patted the boy's knee and waited. And when Manny finally turned, I couldn't stop myself. "Did you see the dog when your dad was on the ground?"

Manny shook his head in tight shudders. Then turned back to the windshield. "I'm not sure, mister. I don't think so. I don't remember. I don't remember much." And a moment later, "Is my dad dead?"

I didn't answer right away. Made a right off of Broadway and then a left into the emergency room traffic circle. Two ambulances—not the ones transporting his father—were unloading patients, so I followed the P signs to the parking garage. Plucked out the ticket from the automatic dispenser. Drove up the ramp to the first open spot and pulled in.

"No, Manny," I said assuming I was lying, "he's not dead."

Manny glared at me. "Not dead?"

"No. At least I don't think so." Then another probable lie: "He was alive when they took him into the ambulance."

The boy spoke in a monotone then: "I think he was dead."

"No, no, no, no," I assured him, patting him on the knee again. "I know for a fact that he was alive when they left for the hospital. They wouldn't have done everything they did if he had already died." Another lie. I frankly had no idea why I was making it all up. To protect the boy? To assure myself that it wasn't my fault? "Let's go inside now and wait for your mom."

Manny seemed to shiver in the unmoving heat of the parking garage and got out of the car.

"You know," I continued, still in the driver's seat, "I don't know where you live."

"Middletown."

"Where?"

"On 138."

"Okay," I said, sliding out of the Jeep, closing the half door, looking all around for a woman I imagined would look like his mom. "She should be here soon, right?"

Manny didn't say anything, so I walked around and put my arm around the boy's shoulders, leading him toward the exit.

Dumbass was out on the sidewalk, lifting his leg and peeing on a sapling. "Is that my dog over there?" I tried, again unable to stop myself.

"No. I don't know."

I pointed with my free hand. "That dog, right up there. Sniffing in the bushes."

Either Manny or I stopped walking then. I frankly still don't know who brought us to a halt, but Manny was mad, "No! I don't see a dog, mister. I don't see a dog. There's no dog! Stop asking me!"

Everything had changed. All I could think to do was grip the boy's shoulder. To breathe in. Breathe out. "I'm sorry, kid. I know you're upset. I shouldn't have—"

"I'm not upset." The boy took a step and then another out of my grasp, striding toward the entrance to the emergency room, not looking back. When I caught up and grasped the boy by the elbow, he repeated, "I am not upset."

"Then what are you?"

His lip was trembling. "I'm hoping the bastard is dead." His eyes were flooding.

"No, you're just upset."

"It's true," he said, walking even faster.

Tempted to explain to Manny that he really didn't hope the old man was dead, that he was traumatized and saying things he didn't mean … or that he'd regret saying later … or something. Something. But I could tell through the force of Manny's pounding footsteps as he swung open and strode through the glass door that it was true. And would never be not true.

"Well," I said, leaning over and speaking just above a whisper, "keep it to yourself for now. Don't say anything about it to your mom or your sister."

"They hate him, too."

I held on to his elbow, making him stop just as we were about to pass the information desk in the lobby; told him to "Wait right here. I gotta get the visitor passes."

The woman behind the desk, Donna DeNunzio, Patient Services, typed R-a-u-l then C-a-r-d-o-z-o into the computer. She glanced up. "I'm not seeing a Raul Cardozo here. Are you sure …?"

I leaned over the counter and under my breath explained that Mr. Cardozo had just been brought in by ambulance.

"Oh, that's why. You'll have to go to the emergency room." She pointed toward the hallway. "Make a right, then a left, and follow signs to Emergency Room. Easy-peasy." She smiled.

I smiled back with some inexplicable affection for the woman I had just met. "Y'know, I'm coming around at this late date to think that nothing in this life is easy-peasy."

"I hear you," she said, still smiling sweetly but a little sadly as well. Manny turned away and was already walking in the direction of the ER; I had to race walk, pumping my arms, to catch up to him. "Whoa, Nellie," I said coming up from behind and once again laying a hand on the boy's shoulder. He didn't stop this time, but I gripped his shoulder tighter as the two of us slowed down and then began walking faster and faster again toward the double doors into the Emergency Room waiting area.

I was out of breath, huffing, puffing, when I heard a woman's voice say, "Manuel! Manuel! *Estamos aqui!*"

A heavyset woman who could be fifty or seventy was waving at us from a glass cubicle. She was sitting next to a younger woman, twenty or so, who was speaking to someone I figured was the intake nurse.

The older woman stood then and held out her chubby arms. Manny ran out from my hand and fell into his mother's embrace, laying his cheek on top of her head.

She said something that sounded Spanish—I figured it was Portuguese—and when she started to wail, Manny placed his hand on her ear and held her against his chest until her sobs subsided, Manny cooing like he'd done it a thousand times before.

I stood behind them feeling helpless. I wanted to explain what I was doing there, but neither mother nor son seemed to acknowledge my hulking, hovering presence. After a few seconds I wandered over to the cubicle and stood behind the girl or woman I assumed was Manny's sister, whose head was bent, nodding.

I tried to chase away the memories of sitting in a different emergency room eighteen years before, after hearing the news of Joni's horrific accident, but the sorrowful words of the surgeon wouldn't leave me alone, a loop as fresh—and searing—as if it all were just happening then, as if no time had passed, as if no time would ever pass: "I'm so sorry, Mr. Messina ..."

Standing there feeling so useless, I knew that this was not a flashback, not a déjà vu, not a memory. The anguish was real and present, and instantly interrupted—actually redirected— by the voice of the intake nurse, asking if I was a family member.

Manny's sister Rosa Cardozo looked up then, her pretty, tear-stained, sculpted face obviously searching my face for some clue as to what I was doing there.

"I'm Charlie Messina," I said. "We spoke on the phone ..."

Rosa smiled so sadly that I thought my heart would break. "Oh yes," she said. "Thank you for taking care of Manny." She pressed her lips together as if she were trying to stem her tears. "Thank you for driving him over here." She nodded to herself and closed her eyes.

And when I glanced at the woman behind the desk, who looked at me with such sad brown eyes that I was now on the verge of wailing myself, I realized that she was not the intake nurse, but Esmerelda Santiago, MSW, Patient Services—and that although I had more or less known that Raul Cardozo had died back at the gas station, it shook me down to the molten core of my very existence to realize that Rosa was not checking Cardozo into ICU, but was instead filling out paperwork for his body to be transported to a funeral home in Middletown.

I turned away then, fully expecting to see Joni standing in the doorway, just as I knew she had been almost there in the living room a few days before. Just as she was when I woke in the hospital. With St. Augustine. And the dog.

But Joni was not there. Nor the other two. This was not about her. Or them. This was not about me. In fact, in that frozen negative of this family's complicated grief, in that darkroom moment when things finally take shape, I understood that nothing in the world is about me.

Nothing.

And in the moments after I felt myself disappearing, I returned to my body and walked over to Manny. The boy, who looked different somehow, was standing alone then, arms at his sides, staring out into the nothingness, his mother leaning back in the chair next to Rosa.

When Manny looked up, I held out my hand. "I'm really sorry, Manny."

Manny didn't take my hand, but said so softly that I'm still not sure I didn't make it up: "It's not your fault."

"No," I said and pressed my lips closed. "But I'm still sorry about your dad. Very sorry."

"I'm not," he whispered. A tear slipped from his right eye.

"It's always complicated, right?"

The boy nodded and then looked away.

My hand was still extended, floating in the air between us. But just as I was going to pull it back and slip it into my pocket, I reached over and grasped Manny's left hand dangling at his side. Squeezed it. "You're a good boy, Manny."

As Manny looked up, I could see a torrent of tears flowing down his cheeks.

"And I really am sorry about your dad."

"Thank you."

I let go of the boy's hand then, but just as he began to pivot away, Manny whispered back, "Mister?"

"What, Manny?"

"There was no dog."

"I know. I know."

And with that, as there was no longer an emergency, I turned away and walked alone toward the Emergency Room exit.

***

When I got back to the parking garage, Dumbass was waiting on the passenger seat. His tail flicked once, twice, when he saw me. "You know where we're going, don't you?"

The dog lowered himself down, his snout on his paws, and shut his eyes.

I shrugged. "Doesn't matter, I guess." I undid the snaps on the rag top, flipped it up and lowered it down into the well. Then opened the half door and slid onto the driver's seat.

Reached across to the open glove box and snared the pack of Luckies. Shook one up, pulled it out between my lips, slipped the pack of matches out of the cellophane, struck the match, sucked in deeply, and, with blasts of smoke coming out between syllables, said, "Well, best friend, let's just drive right into it."

And forty or so minutes later we were pulling into the gravel lot at Gertie's Roadside Rest.

It was a muggy, overcast day, no wind, storm clouds to the south. Dumbass jumped out and ran off into the field.

Just as I'd suspected I would, I heard that girlish voice from behind: "Your dog's not s'posed to run around free, Mister. You gotta leash him 'round here."

My eyes still fixed on Dumbass running out to the tree line, I smiled and said, "You got yourself a lot of goddamn rules, kid."

The boy didn't respond. His long-lashed eyelids fluttered and four-five-six seconds later, I turned to see whether he was still there. Of course, he was. When our eyes met, Joey said, "I keep telling you, mister, that you're not s'posed to take the Lord's name in vain. It just ain't right."

"Right," I said. This moment seemed to me the very confluence of everything that was going on in my life. "I keep forgetting."

Joey scrunched up his lips and swung them to the side as if he didn't know how to respond to this new turn of events. "You want me to get the dog for you, mister, and bring him back here?"

"And what?"

A squiggle of a smile rippled across his dirty face. "Well, maybe you'll pay me for going all the way out there and bringing the dog back so the dogcatcher won't, you know ..." He shrugged and opened his eyes wide.

I laughed out loud, a guffaw the likes of which I only shared with Mason—and then only between months of scowls. "That what your mom does when she's scolding you?"

The boy glared at him. "I dunno. I just thought maybe you didn't wanna walk all the way out there and get yourself all tired out"—the smile reappearing in the pause—"and ... um, I could do it ... and you could pay me or, y'know, something."

"Something?"

"Yup, something ..." he said and then added, as if he'd just thought of it, "another hot-fudge sundae?"

Now it was my turn to glare, but of course I was just playing with the kid—and it was working. The boy's face grew red and his eyes became a little glassy. I pointed my finger between the kid's eyes. "Hey, don't you wimp out on me and start crying."

That brought him back. "I ain't crying. I'm sweating. It's hot."

"Okay. Tell you what I'm gonna do. Forget about the dog. You'll have to trust me on this one; there's no one who is going to bother with that old mutt." He nodded. Then I reached into my pocket and pulled out a couple of twenties. I held one up in the air.

Eyes even wider, Joey reached for it, but I pulled back. "I'm not just giving it to you. You gotta work for it. It's probably worth three or four hot-fudge sundaes, don't ya think?"

The boy licked his lips and sat up straight on the banana seat. He glanced over to the take-out window.

"Is your mom in there working?"

Joey shook his head. "Nope. Not now. She hadda run out to get something for Mr. Chet."

"Who's in there now?"

"I dunno, some girl from the high school. Martha."

"Okay, good. You go over there and buy me a lobster roll ... and then bring it back here, and I just got one question for you."

"What?"

"Get the lobster roll and then I'll ask you the question."

A minute later, a chunky high-school girl was leaning out of the window, following Joey's finger pointing at me. I waved at the girl. "It's okay, dear," I called out, "I'm just having a little trouble walking, and the boy's going to get the lobster roll for me." She gave me a funny look. "It's okay, I'm gonna tip him."

That seemed to make it okay. She smiled and waved back—and five minutes later, Joey was returning holding the paper basket in both hands. Dumbass was back in the Jeep.

"Thank you." I took the roll from the boy. "Change?"

Joey sneered and pulled a clumsy wad of bills from his pocket—and when I gestured, he handed the bills over and then dug in deeper for the change.

"Okay. Now ... for those hot-fudge sundaes." I held up the twenty again. "I want you to reach into the back seat and pet the dog."

Joey shot a glance into the back seat as if he were noticing the dog for the first time. "That's it?"

"Better still," I added, plucking a small piece of lobster from the roll, "give him this."

Joey shrugged and took the slippery, mayonnaise-y piece of lobster meat, held it up over the door, and lowered it to the dog's snout.

Smelling something, Dumbass raised his eyes and, barely leaning forward, gently took the meat from the boy's opened palm. Swallowed it whole, licked his lips, and yawned.

I watched the whole thing intently, each action flowing from the previous one and leading to the next as Joey took his hand back and wiped it on his shorts. Held out his open palm.

"Good. Very good, actually." I extended the twenty and Joey snatched it away, yanking up the front tire of his bike, swiveling the bike around, and pedaling furiously off up Route 6 as if he were being chased by the boogie man.

I didn't follow him this time.

I finished off the lobster roll with two big mouthfuls. Ground the gears putting the Jeep into reverse, listened appreciatively, as I always did, to the whine of the engine. Waited for the westbound traffic on Route 6 to pass. Made a right and, pushing the RPMs to the red line, headed back to Newport. And Sarah. And Dylan. Andrew. Cecilia. Jack and Diane. Mason. The series about Joey and Manny that I'd been working on—and now thought I knew why. At least as much as anyone knows anything.

PART VI

"Déjà vu all over again."
—Yogi Berra

Chapter Twenty-One (Later or your guess is as good as mine)

So now I'm back in the studio some time later, once again growling at the dog for humping my leg at the Calvin Theater. "It's goddamn bad manners and it makes me look like I'm some kind of doddering old spastic trying to get you off of me."

A second or a lifetime later the dog has disappeared, once again not having walked the conventional way through the doorway and down the hall going wherever he might be going. No. As I instantly understand, have seemingly understood always, Dumbass has simply stepped through the veil, "another caul," I correct myself, knowing he will return when he again has something to say to me—or maybe more correctly, not say. This is no talking dog.

I return to the series on Joey, Manny, Jack, and Diane, contact sheets spread around the work table, jeweler's glass in my eye. Not one shot of the dog. I feel myself press my lips together and then say out loud to the dog as if the dog were there, "This is all of a piece ... but I guess I'm gonna have to put it out there and see what it is. What it is ..."

Just then, a knock on the doorframe to the studio. Dylan. Standing like da Vinci's *Vitruvian Man*, clothed of course but feet spread and both hands extended, each pressed into the opposite door jamb. Talk about déjà vu. *This is beginning to feel really ridiculous,* I think.

"Hey, old man." Dylan smirks at his own yet-to-be-spoken joke. Then he tilts his head like he's going to say something he knows I won't like.

"Yeah, hey ... and what tidings of comfort and joy you bringing for me?"

"Got some news, big news, good news," he says and pauses, perhaps waiting for me to ask him to go on.

"Go on," I say, smiling, frankly more relieved than anxious to hear of some triumph rather than another whine in my grown son's life. "Shoot." But something's not right. This feels out of sequence. Before he can answer and before I can censor myself, I ask, "Isn't this early?"

He shrugs, as clueless as I am. "Nope. Actually right on time ..." Then with another smile awkwardly stifling a laugh, "BadBreath just got a major gig ... long story short, but there was a late cancellation and now we're headlining at the October BuckyFest out in Madison, Wisconsin, and—"

I cut him off right on cue: "BuckyFest? What in the hell is a Buckyfest? An orthodontist convention?"

"Jesus Christ, Charlie, just fuckin' listen—"

"Don't call me Charlie," I shoot back, but then quickly flash a smile that feels perilously close to exploding into a wail when I understand where we're going. "Sorry, son," I begin reciting my lines, "I am officially stopping being a Class A pain in the ass right now. So, tell me ..."

Dylan raises his eyebrows in stunned disbelief. "Okay. Not sure what's going on with you, but it's a big-time fall concert series—like, hmmmm, Saratoga?" He pauses then, but the imminent wailing disappears and now I just don't understand. "Bonnarroo?" he tries. I shrug. "Burning Man?" Another shrug. "Okay ... Newport Folk Festival?"

"Yup." *Of course.*

"Well, like I said, this is a big deal—a really big deal for the band—and we were wondering, I was wondering, if you—and maybe you and Mason—want to go along to be our documentarians?"

Instantly slung around by ricocheting emotions, back and forth between worlds, between love and fear, then and now, in the spaces between the everything that seems to be true and all the things I know to be true, I am speechless.

In that perilous moment I know precisely what it means to go out there. And in the midst of the shredded linen membrane behind my eyes, I know in my heart I have no choice but to go.

So, I hear myself saying this: "Holy crap, Dylan, that's pretty damn wonderful!"

And I'm grinning, like I used to do as a boy gliding around Milford on my bike, like I did years before, at the boy who grew to the man filling the doorway. "Even if I don't know what the hell a BuckyFest is really all about."

"It's the next Woodstock, Dad. It's hopefully a celebration of the end of that piece of shit in the White House's reign of terror. And we're the ones bringing it to a glorious end."

I step through the caul and say, "I couldn't miss it for the world."

"Wouldn't, you mean."

"Wouldn't, couldn't, same thing." Then I add, "I'll tear Mason away from whatever widow he's currently charming out of her knickers and we'll meet you out there. You can count on it."

CPSIA information can be obtained
at www.ICGtesting.com
Printed in the USA
JSHW041736180322
23963JS00002B/107